About the Author

Gregory Baines lives just outside Canberra, Australia. He has an arts degree from Newcastle University. He lived in China for thirteen years, where he also met his wife. There he wrote his first novel and had short stories published in anthologies and online.

The Nail House

GREGORY BAINES

Fairlight Books

First published by Fairlight Books 2019

Fairlight Books
Summertown Pavilion, 18-24 Middle Way, Oxford, OX2 7LG

A CIP catalogue record for this book is available from the
British Library

1 2 3 4 5 6 7 8 9 10

ISBN 978-1-912054-96-1

www.fairlightbooks.com

Printed and bound in Great Britain

Designed by Sara Wood
Illustrated by Sam Kalda
www.folioart.co.uk

For Huang Yan Ting (Jen), Vy and Lyam Baines.
My words, small slices of my heart,
belong to you three.

I

'If you know the enemy and know yourself, you need not fear the result of a hundred battles. If you know yourself but not the enemy, for every victory gained you will also suffer a defeat. If you know neither the enemy nor yourself, you will succumb in every battle.'
The Art of War, Sun Tzu, Chapter 3, 18

Zhen

Even from here, three blocks away, I can feel the small shockwaves from the school as the walls crash down. It's one of the last buildings to be demolished, the chalk-stained, white-washed walls in which I completed my schooling. Dust is dislodged in my room, it drifts in small currents towards the window. I have lived here, in my parents' house, forever. I'm itching to leave. I want to fly away.

The door still has my name carved in it from my school days: Zhen Yi. If you are a foreigner reading this, you say my name 'Jen Ee'. My parents have already stuck the red 'double happiness' paper cut-out above my name even though the wedding is weeks away.

I feel the lightness of the bag in my hand. It's ready to be filled with memories from here. My fiancé, Sun, will come tonight after work to pick me up and we will spend our first night in the tiny flat with flaking walls we have rented across the city. This will all be an open secret, of course: something everyone knows is happening, but no one talks about. We can't officially start living together until our wedding night. Sun said he will borrow his cousin's car, an old VW Santana that breaks down more often than it completes a trip, to rescue me from my parents.

My mother is trying to paper over her sadness about me going, and the avalanche of other things. She shoves food at me as I go back out into the living room. She has made tea in her chipped enamel cups. I say no to the food. It looks reheated and dead. She doesn't seem to have the energy to cook fresh food each day now. She looks pale, too thin, like the part of her I know is wilting. She says she is glad the school is gone; she says it was old and mouldy. But her eyes betray a different feeling. There are no more shockwaves now.

My father is by the front window cleaning up glass, sweeping it up into an old cracked red dustpan. Someone smashed the front window last night, using a broken piece of concrete. The lights reflected from the glass buzz around him, flies round the dying. Last week they jammed pig shit in the guttering. The week before that they burnt my mother's clothes. That was the last straw for her; that was when she passed out for the first time.

The property company desperately want us gone.

Ours is the last house left on-site undemolished. My father has turned our house into what we call a 'nail house'. It is the name given to a family's home, when the owners are offered money to move so that it can be demolished, but they refuse to leave. It's a pun that refers to nails that are stuck in wood, and can't be pulled out. My father is the nail. We have even been in the papers. Photos of my father on the roof, defiantly pelting attackers with rocks. He is our family's greatest embarrassment. He has some old-fashioned idea about this being 'his home' but it's just a sad, sagging old building that needs tearing down. Some of our family friends have already moved into new flats across town, with air con and sealed windows. I had respect for my father when I thought he was just hanging out for a better compensation package, but I despaired when he started ranting about 'our rights'.

The tea burns my lip. I blow gently across the steaming surface of the liquid and watch my mother through the fog. She goes to the kitchen to wash up and I can see her from here. Her hands are shaking. I tell her to stop but she ignores me. My father does nothing; I can hear the sound of shattered glass scratching across the concrete floor like gnashing dragon's teeth as he continues to sweep, lost in his own battle. I sigh and leave my tea as I head for the kitchen to stop my mother washing up. I look at the clock, willing it forwards. In a few hours Sun will rescue me from all this shit.

Lindon

How could I end up somewhere so grey, so cold, cocooned in concrete and smog at the end of the world? I close my eyes against an icy gust of wind and I see her nasty smile. The image tightens my stomach, brings the anger up into my throat. The end of a relationship haunts you in ways other things don't; it hounds you through the beginnings of your new life. China seemed to be the best place to forget Julie's face, somewhere far enough away, big enough – where a bankrupt person can work off their debt.

I open my eyes. They don't seem to understand my English and I don't understand them, but they smile nonetheless, with their cigarette-stained teeth and touched-up carbon-fibre black hair.

It has started to snow. It settles on our coats like icing sugar on puff pastry. I look up constantly at the small stage next to us to see if we will begin soon, but there's only a lonely microphone there now.

We are outside our office building in the city, my seventh day in China; seven days of semi-comprehensible ceremonies and planning meetings. We stomp around in hats and gloves and heavy coats trying to keep warm, but I am optimistic today – this is the official start of the project, the start of what I hope will be actual work. I gaze up at a banner above the stage with the company name 'Golden Double Lucky Property Group' printed across it, and below that 'Making luxury home future first-class world in modern harmonious China' for all to see, with its lost articles and muddy meaning.

Finally, three beautiful girls in long red traditional dresses and high heels wobble up on stage and we are pointed at, the translator and I, beckoned to join them. We clamber up and stand to the right of the pretty girls while others file on stage to the left; one of them is the CEO. I've only seen his photograph in the city offices, above the front entrance, as a young man smoking cigarettes with a former Premier, the one-time head of the country. The image is blown up to garish proportions, maybe a metre wide – a totem of power. It arrests you as you walk in, presses you down, reminding you how powerful he is. The white man from over the ocean who smoked cigarettes with Jiang Zemin isn't to be fucked with.

Suits move forwards with more urgency to the ribbon, cigarettes hanging out of the corners of their mouths. Lazy, precarious columns of ash jut out at angles and make grey smudges on the shoulders of their jackets. The CEO holds a pair of scissors up high, the metallic edges catching the sunlight, and he brings them down like he's slaughtering an animal, offering up a sacrifice. The ribbon falls to the ground with no cheers, just the crescendo of a band's rhythm and some lukewarm clapping – classic corporate propaganda.

I thought this would all be so simple, and would come cheaply, but everything has its price.

*

Zhen

It's good to see Sun for a change. Why are we here? My bags are bulging with objects ready for our flat. But he has told me that can wait, that he wants to show me an 'exciting development' first. Our plan was to buy our own apartment close to my parents in the city, to buy a place in a block adjoining the new development. Instead we are here, on the edge of town, on the edge of civilisation. Sun doesn't listen.

More queues. Small kids play alongside with their toys, bored old people squat. They put down newspapers and sit on them. Above us a giant billboard is stretched out, and flaps softly in the wind. Two perfect-looking people with digitally altered white teeth and no blemishes stand with an impossibly cute child. They live in the completed development in some indefinite future. It has made them happy, four walls and a roof. The woman's breasts look like they have been stretched. Everyone around them smiles like they are in an American movie, and the sky is blue. Blue in blue, fluffy white clouds. We see blue skies like these two or three weeks a year.

Perhaps that's why they have the imported smiles.

Sun has bought snacks. He slides them out of his bag and starts cracking open nuts, throws the shells at his feet. He peels a small handful and offers them to me. He does it quickly, excitedly. I take one. It's dry and flavourless. It gets stuck in my teeth and I spit the rest out.

He is looking through the leaflet, like everyone else. Pages flap in the breeze in people's hands. Some blow away down the line towards the street.

I don't know what to say to him; he feels thousands of miles away, even as we touch. I'm thinking of my full bags at my parents' place, bulging with the possibility of a new freedom with Sun.

'I like the north block,' he says, spitting some husks out onto the ground at his feet. 'There are still some good floor plans left.' He looks at the queue. He knows that a great deal depends on how quickly we make it to the front. Lots of the ones we like will have been sold by the time we get there.

'These are better,' I throw in, irritated. I'm watching the leaflets blow into the street and my eyes follow one that gets picked up by a gust of wind and drifts back into a farmer's field next door. This development is on farmland, rising from a peasants' village that's being demolished. I scan the city on the horizon. Every side of this development is framed by wheat fields and some rice. I can smell animals on the wind. Maybe pigs. No one seems to look into the farms, they all have their heads stuck in their brochures.

They are all dreaming of high-rises, the future not the present.

Sun speaks, excitement lacing his words, 'There will be a small shopping area built on the east side, and two more developments the other side.' He knows I'm wondering why we are here, but doesn't want to answer the question.

I let the wind take my pamphlet; it flutters away. 'This is not what we agreed. I don't want to be a farmer.'

He sighs, puts his arm round me. He is blushing at my very public directness. 'We couldn't get a place this size in the city.' He smiles more to the people around us than me. To cover his loss of face.

I nod, watching a farmer cycle out to a spot in a wheat field. It all looks the same to me but he must know why it is different from everywhere else. He stops and gets something out of a bag. It looks to be a long tool of some kind. He starts to attack the earth.

'We are getting in at the right time...' Sun must be looking at me for a reply. I sense it in his silence. The knowing of lovers.

I say, 'Yes, good time.' But a feeling of being pressed down, weighed down by concrete, descends. Our marriage is being anchored in concrete, confused by it. I want to go home.

He squints at me. 'You seem to be thinking about something else. I thought you'd be happy.'

'I am,' I say, trying to keep my irritation from getting out.

'This is where our baby will be,' he says. I have small snapshots in my head of our future life, but they seem to be fading. The colour is blurring. Wedding nerves.

I touch his leg. 'Don't you think it's a little cold?' He rummages for a light jacket, drapes it on my shoulders. I let my shoulders slump under it. I pick at the edges of a nail that has split. 'I hate queues. You know that.'

He examines my face, not convinced.

The queue starts to shorten. Sun draws some ideas on a couple of the plans, and we discuss what designs would be good. 'That will be good for the baby...', 'That will be good for our parents...', 'We should focus on decorating like xxx here...'. I agree, seeing the good all these would do everyone.

A couple of families leave, frustrated with the long wait. Or perhaps they've heard that the place they wanted has been sold?

We are in the showroom at last. Three large models are buried in a glass box like jewels made of foam. People in purple suits with laser pointers stand around looking bored or hungry or both. They flash the lights around, to show what apartments are left. I hear a lot of talk about price. These are cheap places.

Sun elbows his way in closer to the model, starts matching the plans to the model. His eyes hunt the small doll's house-like windows. He turns round.

He has taken a laser pointer and starts directing my eyes to various features, dragging me closer to the model and out of my daydream. 'That would be good for us, for the kids. Our parents would like the way it faces.'

'It would please everyone.' I have a fantasy, just for a moment, like I've never had before. In this fantasy I back away while Sun is preoccupied and slip through the people and run.

I run through fields of wheat, disappearing to find my own potholed road after stealing the peasant's bicycle.

*

Lindon

I'm hung-over from the third formal welcome dinner for me in the last several days. My throat is dry and my clothes smell of a meal of hot pot and *baijiu*, a potent head-splitting white spirit. I squeeze out of the taxi into a bloom of humanity and by the time I am upright and ready to walk away from the kerb someone has jumped into the cab and it is away again. I thread through people and pass between two bicycles, both with fruit laid out for sale on large metal trays attached behind the seats, my head pounding with each footstep like there is a direct line from my feet to my brain. I sidestep a beggar in blue jeans and Nike shoes who smells of mould and pushes a small dented disposable cup full of old coins at me. I need all my change and so I ignore him, pretend I haven't seen him.

A glass cube stuck to the outside of our office building hauls me away from the mess below. I notice a couple holding hands in the throng and I watch them as the lift ascends, wondering if I will ever be able to forget the scars Julie has left and be able to do that again with someone.

The American CEO is standing waiting for me, an age-scarred version of the young man in the image with the former Premier. He shakes my hand so hard the bones in my fingers creak under the strain and I wonder if he shook the Premier's hand like that, wonder if he dared.

We go to the boardroom, a space almost completely devoid of concrete walls – it's just curtains of glass on never-ending city. The carpet has probably just been rolled out in here because it hasn't even been attached to the floor; I can see it turns at the corners and sides.

I have borrowed all I can – stretched the goodwill of my family and friends to the limit just to get here – and I'm anxious to get my signature down on the contract so I can start paying people back. But I forget all that for a moment and allow myself to be distracted by the view; it's overwhelming, engulfing. The CEO notices and says, 'It's quite a city isn't it?' and I nod, trying to obscure my hunger. An old grey landscape is being swept away by piles of glass, steel and concrete stacked up by hundreds of cranes. It's mesmerising and my heart starts to pound when I think of the money to be made here, the staggering numbers that must lie beneath me.

His secretary comes in. She looks perfect, newly minted, like she has just come out of a box on a shelf. She tilts her head and smiles at me but doesn't stop to talk – I'm part of a task she must perform, nothing more.

A large model of the apartment complex sits in the corner of the new office: the completed foam replica of the apartments we will build twenty storeys into the sky. It looks small after my last job, like a toy. The CEO sees me looking over at the model and he waves me over towards it. From a distance it looks like a perfect miniature of the real thing, but as we get closer I see plastic edges, sloppy paint and that it is fragile and cheap.

He begins to talk me through some figures on the number of apartments and their expectations but he is interrupted. Some locals in suits come to the door, ask to speak to him. He speaks for a while in Chinese that, to my untrained ear, sounds as good as that of the locals he is talking to, then excuses himself from me and turns to go.

I put out my hand, touch his sleeve, my anxiety spilling out. 'The contract, is it ready to sign?'

He smiles, glances down at my hand. 'It's being finalised now, but if you have some settling-in tasks to do, you can come back this afternoon or tomorrow morning.'

I try to curb my impatience, keep a smile on my face, slow my voice down. 'I may as well sign it now, I can wait here.'

He nods and points in the direction of a meeting room where he says my contract will be delivered in a little while. He says there is a pile of magazines in there, and then he strides away from me engrossed in his next conversation.

I take a wrong turn, end up at the doorway to another office. A lady in a black suit sits opposite a shorter woman who is crying – tears roll down her cheeks and drip off her chin. I stand, shocked, for a second; I don't know what to say. The woman in black points in the other direction and pushes the door shut on me. I don't understand what I have just seen. I'm trying to survive each day blindfolded and I'm stumbling ahead one step at a time.

The CEO's secretary is in the meeting room. She has a thick wad of paper wedged in her hands. I stare at it, hoping it's my contract and she looks up at me and says, 'Mr Lin, we are ready.'

'It's Lindon,' I correct her, my eyes on the sheaf of papers.

She laughs but her eyes are focussed on something over my shoulder. 'Mr Lin, please step inside so we can deal with the documents.' She motions for me to enter the room and I step towards her and settle into a seat opposite, leaning forwards eagerly. She lays the document down between us, the tips of her fingers resting on it. Her nails are painted a thick glossy red.

She looks at me, the smile gone. I reach forwards to pull the document towards me but her fingers press down and the document is stuck between us.

She says quietly, 'There are certain formalities that we must discuss first.'

'Of course.'

'This is China, so one of the documents you will be signing here requires you to be aware that your contract will be terminated if you violate the laws and morals of the People's Republic of China.' I pull a little harder on the document but she doesn't release it. She asks, 'Are you aware of what this means?'

I'm not but I don't care. I say, to dodge more lengthy unnecessary talk, 'Yes, of course.'

She lifts her fingers and I pull the document towards me, start flicking through the pages. She anticipates me and as I look up to ask for it, she slides across a black pen. She makes no eye contact, she is already lost in her mobile phone, on to a new person, a new task.

I scribble in signatures where required, ignoring all the fine print, ignoring all the conditions. The only figure I check is the monthly salary and bonus. I smile as I finish and slide the documents eagerly across the table. I sit back, relieved. I have not disguised how much I need the job with my eagerness.

The numbers in the contract have so many zeros I forget my hangover, the jackhammers in my head. As I rise to leave, smiling stupidly, she says she has to tell me something else. She slides the meeting room door closed and shuffles a chair next to mine as I sit back down. I can smell her perfume, it's strong and flowery. She leans towards me and begins to tell me about nail houses.

The lift seems to take an age to get to the ground floor. I stare at the floor working through what I have just learnt, feel the weight of it bearing down on me. I find myself, naively, looking for the couple holding hands but I see instead people alone, their hands in their pockets, their eyes far away.

II

Zhen

I have been in this bar so many times, it's like reading the same book again and again. The pages are grubby and hold no surprises. I'm here alone tonight, hoping beer will wash away my irritation with Sun.

My head feels like it's being split with each bass thud. Makes it hard to think. DJs all sound the same. Just different posters. Stupid names – DJ Missile, DJ Jam.

Each drink I purchase is studied, timed. I switch to cognac from the cheap beer. I work out that each glass of cognac costs me four point one hours of my meagre wages. This is not to be taken lightly. But I don't care any more. It relaxes me, softens the pounding in my head. The bartender pours a small stain of four hours' labour into my glass. I wince. Here's to my family-friendly fiancé who has been so busy at work I've been stuck at my parents' for two long extra days. He thinks his meetings with his boss are more important than moving me into our flat.

I swig another small mouthful of brandy and message my friend Mei to see how she is. But there is no reply.

Some cheap-looking girl moves in front of me and eyes a foreigner. She must think I'm competition, but I don't have the required layers of make-up. I wear jeans, not a short skirt. And I don't like foreign men, not like that. The foreigner smiles at her, doesn't see me. His eyes move down her legs to her high heels. We are playthings to them. He is like a child.

The cheap girl, whose heels are more like school-made stilts, stumbles onto my toes causing a sharp stab of pain. Worse, I see in a quick machine-gun fire of strobe that she's stained the toes of my favourite shoes. I try to push her away but end up stumbling myself. Too much cognac and out-manoeuvred, I fall off my stool and onto my feet, but kick out at her as I do. Mud that always seems to be caked to the bottom of my shoes stains her clothes, makes me smile. My handbag strikes the foreigner on the side. He doesn't notice though; he is too busy trying to scoop up the heeled painted doll falling at his feet. He looks like a baby happy with his cheap breakable toy. You get what you pay for, right?

I feel more lost than when I arrived. Drinking has clouded me. I feel like I'm sinking inside. More music, too loud. I have to get out so I head towards the flood of light spilling from the exit. There are lots of people between me and the coat rack. I'm going through my pockets looking for the tag. Hair is in my eyes, sticky with sweat. People behind wait for me, watching.

A foreigner stumbles forwards to the head of the queue, with a small group around him. I can't see his face clearly. He has sandy-coloured hair that was once styled in some sort of business cut, but it's now slightly overgrown. I see a flash of dark eyes. His clothes look cheap, but I notice an expensive pair of shoes, one of the brands Mei goes on about. He looks bored, numb. He's too drunk or too clueless to see a system and pushes in front of me.

'Wait, join the queue. They are getting my coat.' I feel blood rush to my cheeks as I say this, want to rewind that last moment and keep my mouth shut. I must have drunk too much, I am never so direct with strangers.

He mutters, 'Doesn't even seem to be a queue, don't know how you can tell.'

I push hair out of my face, fold my arms. 'Foreigners often miss the obvious.'

He rocks back on his heels now, steadies himself on the counter. I see him examine my face. The group with him has drifted off towards the door. He doesn't seem to care. 'I've fucked up. I…' He looks down at his shoes, takes one hand out to steady himself against the wall near him. He splutters, 'I didn't mean it quite like that…' The words run together like ink. I wince at the toxic smell of what he has drunk; I can smell it from where I am.

I pull back a little. 'I don't talk to drunks.' I regret starting this, look over his shoulder willing someone to come back with my coat. I fold my arms and stand there, hoping I can escape quickly. My bravery is evaporating.

He grunts, points his finger at me, trying to end the tense silence between us. 'You know… I've seen no system in this city so far… crazy drivers, brave cyclists…'

He stops pointing when he realises I won't respond. People are looking and I just want to go home now. He turns away from me, sighs, runs his hands through his hair, says, 'Sorry.' I glance at him: he looks lost. I feel a flicker of pity for him.

I mutter, 'You'll feel better tomorrow.' He doesn't reply.

Someone comes with my coat and I take it from her, anxious to flee. In my haste I stumble, and the foreigner lurches to help me, grabs my arm. I jump away and move towards the door. I feel the air from the outside smother the sound from the club behind me. It shrinks it to a monotone.

He follows me outside. I stumble to the front of a taxi queue and try to muscle my way into a taxi to get away from him. I hear him from behind me, 'There's a system, get in line…' His interruption has prevented me from being pushed by three women I have offended by trying to take their place in the taxi queue. He looks happy seeing this revenge and leads me away before they vent their rage at me.

'I'd buy you a drink, to say sorry, but I don't have any money left,' he says.

He must be lying. 'How can a foreigner not have money?' I grunt.

He smiles, looks at my shoes. 'Well, not all of us have money to burn.'

I should walk away, but I don't, I stand on the edge of the street neither in a queue for a taxi nor walking away. I can't explain why I don't want to move or why half of me prevents the other half from doing so, a stalemate. I say, 'Well, you must have something, you couldn't have swum here from your country.'

I hope he will walk away, but he chuckles. I see a flash of those eyes and I look down at the pavement. He says, 'My company paid for the ticket and set me up, so... no great swimming skills.' He tries to say something else but the wind picks up and we both recoil as the cold hits us.

We shuffle back away from the road towards the door where there is some shelter. I notice, with enough light now from the lantern in the doorway, that he is unshaven. 'You don't need to buy me a drink, I'm used to foreigners.'

He raises his eyebrows. 'Used to arrogance?'

'Yes.' My cheeks flush and I turn away from him, my arms folded and pressed against my breasts to hold the warmth in.

'Funny,' he says, 'I was just thinking *you* were arrogant.' I grit my teeth, want to yell at him but I am incapable of even grasping at an English word to respond.

He finds a business card and thrusts it at me. 'Well, I should give this to you. They say that's the right thing to do here.' I feel my eyebrows arch. Such thick skin; 'the nerve', as they say in foreign movies. It says 'Golden Dragon Property' above his name, Lindon. He works for *them*.

I snatch it quickly, my upbringing forbidding me from leaving it in his hands. I pull too hard and he topples forwards, almost falls to the street. I leave, turning my back on him, and head for the subway as rain starts to fall. I only get a few metres from him when he yells, 'What's your name?'

I wonder why he cares. I stop and turn round. Rain starts to prick my face with icy water and I breathe hard. 'Zhen Yi.' The rain gets heavier and I rush away.

As the subway entrance looms up in front of me I look back and see he is following me. I notice, in the rain that's fanning out on the road, that the mud from his shoes is leaving a trail behind him. He looks like a child, a large clumsy child. I begin to laugh, a real laugh. I'm more in the habit of 'show faces' and deceitful body language. That is my life. Smile to the right people, strategic emotional display. But this laugh is real. I slip his card into a pocket, careful to remember where I put it, and disappear into the subway.

Later, on the platform, I see him squinting in the glare of fluorescent light. We don't talk. He has retreated into himself anyway, is far away. I turn to go to my end of the platform and am happy that a train glides in right away. I don't look at him again; I just turn and disappear into the carriage.

My phone begins screeching. It's Sun; I see his name on the screen and I'm relieved to hear from him. I want to hear his voice after everything that's gone on tonight. It has flushed out the frustration. Was I a bitch to him? Should I be a more supportive fiancée? There are ads for bras opposite me. Sun sounds perfect, as usual, his voice deep and calm. He apologises for being out so late again. He has signed a big new contract. Says this one will 'change everything' but I've heard this before.

I say, 'I'm not feeling well, baby. I need to be in our own place. My parents are driving me crazy…' I listen to his voice; my toe aches from the club. The foreigner's smile is everywhere I look in the subway. It's the only thing I can see and I feel terrible for this small emotional betrayal. I don't even know why I would think about that stupid, arrogant man.

As the train gathers speed heading away from the station, Sun is saying, '…and you should make sure you keep warm, it's starting to rain they say, and I hope you were careful with—' but as the train enters a tunnel we lose our signal.

His voice disappears mid-sentence and my shoulders go slack. I sink back against the door.

I look forward to being surrounded by his presence, smelling his skin. But I won't see him again tonight; I will be at my parents'.

When I get off at my stop, the rain has started to descend in heavy sheets. At home I clear my pockets. All the paper has formed a soft mess of running ink and pulp. There is no number left. I'm relieved about this, almost happy.

Why would I want some stuck-up foreign man's phone number anyway?

*

Lindon

I have been hired much like a mascot on a sports team to smile and drink and show my face at ceremonies, not to actually work. I have the foam model in my head, but there is no 'nail house' on the model so I have escaped today, slipped out of a press conference between camera flashes and toasting glasses and managed to get a taxi; we are speeding out across an endless overpass towards the site, Chinese news blaring over the car's speakers. I must get a look at this nail house for myself, size it up and give them their marching orders.

I sit in the back, squashed in with the young guy they have provided as a translator, whose eyes are permanently attached to his mobile phone. I don't know his name and he doesn't seem to care too much to know mine. I notice another taxi travels the whole way then pulls in a block ahead of us when we arrive, and I wonder, in a made-for-TV moment, if I am being followed. I watch an old guy get out of the taxi, clutching a shopping bag, and wander off ahead to a small row of shops in the distance but he doesn't look back.

I leave paranoid thoughts behind and stride across the road through the torn muddy shreds of earth left in machines' wakes. A blue steel construction fence has enveloped the site. Old apartment blocks remain as visible reminders of how much we will improve this place with developments like this one. I duck under a loosely chained driveway in the centre front next to the company logo and I smile to myself as the translator trips on a rise of mud as he texts and walks – serves him right.

Once inside I stop, trying to take in what I see, startled. This construction rises out of two deep round pits; behind, in the distance, is a block of apartments that have – on the plans at least – already been removed, but they are still partially standing. People come in and out of the entrance, some moving in my direction when they see me wandering further into the site. I see only two cranes installed to service the ten storeys of the building that has currently been started in the pit to the left of me; there should be more machinery, more activity. Workers' accommodation, at least, has been built at the far end of the site, opposite me – small white sheds are piled on top of each other; some sort of makeshift kitchen next to them billows smoke. Some of the bottom sheds have been made with what I assume are the bricks of the houses already demolished.

As I look around men stop in their tracks – one guy stands in front of me to my left and a couple thrust pages at me that are tattered and torn. I ignore them, for the moment taking in the nail house. I'd pictured a house or two standing amongst machinery but this is so much more than that: there is an island of land left in the middle of the second pit, and a narrow land bridge connects it to where I stand.

Sitting on top of the island is a house, a regular terraced house. Other buildings have obviously been demolished around it, but this one has been spared, left intact, and it's perched up on top of the island like a rotten tooth. An old man shuffles around on the roof, piling up stones and rocks. He has red flags flying from makeshift beams of wood that emerge from the corners of the roof. He stops when he sees us and stares in our direction, peers down at us like *we* are somehow the odd ones in this scene. The translator shuffles up beside me, breathing heavily from the short walk, and doesn't seem to be at all taken aback, like what is in front of us is an everyday occurrence.

Voices now attract my attention. I count over a dozen people heading towards me and they all talk at once. One guy has an ill-fitting security uniform on and a jar of tea in his hand. The guard points back at the gate and I shrug and yell, 'I don't understand...' I wave my company ID at them, hope this will scare them off, intimidate them in some way. A dog starts barking from within the house in the pit. The translator looks at me for direction but I shrug again and move closer to the earth bridge that connects the nail house to the edge. The small crowd that has gathered follows me. The translator, I notice as I glance back, looks worried and when we make eye contact he says, 'These are angry local residents. They want to speak to you, but I wouldn't recommend it.'

As I stop on the land bridge itself to take a couple of images with my phone, the translator pulls on my sleeve. 'We should go back, let others deal with this.'

The residents who have followed us start to back up, won't set foot on the bridge. I pull away from the translator and say, 'I just need to let them know a couple of things, I'll be all right.'

He laughs. 'Mister, the on-site office is over that way...' He points back behind us and I notice the small crowd are looking at each other – some smile and I wonder what these smiles mean.

'I won't take long.' I start to walk across the land bridge. No one, including the translator, is moving with me; they stand watching like they are looking at an accident, but this suits me. It makes things less complicated. I notice a camera crew have run up behind the crowd but they keep their distance as well.

As I turn my head from them I look up to seek

out the old man but he seems to have disappeared from sight. It's then that the first projectile hits me. I am lucky that this one is just a ball of mud that strikes my leg and it doesn't hurt too much, but I still stagger a bit with the force and surprise of it. I'm off balance and I lurch towards the side of the land bridge, hands now instinctively over my head waiting for the next blow, and I overbalance at the edge. I hear a collective gasp behind me and look down – the drop must be about twenty metres and I feel my fingers and toes tingle as I pull my weight back the other way to avoid dropping into the pit. I stumble as I do this and end up on my hands and knees.

Mud covers my legs and threatens to stain my only suit. I curse under my breath as another projectile hits my head. It's softer and larger. My legs crumple.

Soft mud cascades down my face and brings me safely down to the ground, where I curse again. I hear laughter from behind and I turn to hurl abuse at my assailants but as I open my mouth the third projectile hits my back and pain shoots up into my neck.

Another harder object hits the ground in front of me as I try to get up, my eyes foggy with mud. It's then I hear a loud woman's voice in front of me yell, 'Stop!'

I wipe mud off my face and it drips down the ends of my fingers. I peer through the grime looking for the source of the voice. I can't see her face under a woollen hat and a hooded jacket.

I can only really see her eyes – they shine somehow out of the cold. She walks from the nail house and the old man trails twenty metres or so behind her, some sort of sharp object still in his hand ready for battle.

Anger overwhelms me, driven by the pain in my back. 'What the fuck was that for?'

The woman comes closer now, pushes back the hood and she is instantly familiar – the girl from the nightclub. She says, 'My father is causing all of us lots of trouble. I'm sorry.'

It takes her a fraction longer to recognise me, but it's there in the way her face tightens as I speak. 'Your father is mad.'

She frowns. 'My father is under a lot of pressure.'

Pain radiates across my back again in a new wave and I wince. 'I just came out to chat with him, not get attacked.'

'My father was the one that attacked you, talk to him.' She turns to leave.

'I assume that animal behind you is your father?'

Zhen stops, spins round. 'Don't call my father names, drunk.'

'Drunk?' Mud is trickling into the corners of my mouth, it's gritty in my teeth.

I sneer, happy this has offended her, 'You're just lucky I don't get the police out here.'

Zhen whistles and I hear the dog bark again. It appears from a hole in the wall at the front of her home and races towards me. I grin despite the pain, pretend the dog doesn't frighten the piss out of me. 'Calling out your attack dogs?' I jeer.

She stands opposite me, impassive, and the dog, much to my relief, stops beside her. I look back, smiling. The film crew have advanced onto the land bridge and are still recording. I notice a brand name on the side of the camera that suggests a local news station so I consider my next words carefully. I clear my throat, straighten my muddy tie, push muddy hair out of my face and say, 'Well, I won't bill you for the dry cleaning I'll need.'

I hold out my hand to pressure the girl into a handshake, but the dog darts forwards and sinks its teeth into my calf. There is excited chatter from the crowd behind and no one stops to help. I curse, trying to flick the dog away with my hand but only the translator comes forwards to make an effort and the dog lets go of me to lash out at him. I launch a kick at the dog but my other foot slips in the mud and I end up landing on my backside.

The jolt aggravates the pain in my back but scares the dog. I hear clapping from the now excited audience behind.

I keep my voice calm for the cameras, try my best to smile. When I look up at Zhen I notice she is holding her hand over her obviously grinning mouth and I say through gritted teeth, 'Just remind your father he only has another forty-eight hours to leave. We are behind schedule already and this building won't stop for him or anyone else.'

Zhen turns and marches away, obviously filled with contempt and hate for me, yet I have sent her a clear strong message; at least I have that satisfaction. I get up slowly, fighting pain and mud. How are we going to fill this shitty fucking hole with the promises of the foam model?

I get to the road, the crowd stare and laugh at me with my muddy suit and hair and I see the man with the shopping bag watching me from across the street. He smiles at me. He looks like an ordinary person, but he has perfectly straight white shining teeth and he nods his head at me when we make eye contact.

*

Zhen

As I open the front door the sound of mah-jong tiles signals home, rest. I see a note folded and jammed in the side of the door. I unfold it, and black dust falls from it as it opens. I scan it quickly as I move inside – it confirms the deadline to 'evacuate' ready for demolition. Lindon's signature is scrawled on the bottom, in wild looping letters. It's a frail, dusty piece of paper, but it contains so much power. I pick it up and peer at it in the brittle light again as I move inside, look more closely, see a large number on it. He has increased the amount of compensation. He is trying to buy us off. I feel like we are an item on his spreadsheet now. My father notices me looking at the paper but doesn't say anything.

Sun's dad starts sorting through the mah-jong tiles. That sound, the feeling of family that it triggers, makes it nice to be home despite the mud I have had to walk through. I go to the kitchen, let the note fall back on the table. Our family's bright future in numbers. It's my job to make my father accept this. But it feels too cheap, not enough money.

Sun's father is drinking tea. I can hear the two of them, Sun's and my father, from the kitchen, the warmth in their voices. They chat quietly. For a while it's talk about property prices and the new compensation figure. I try and eavesdrop but they keep quiet so my mother doesn't hear. Then the conversation brightens a little, something about the price of food, and then it blends into 'the old days'. They occasionally chuckle. I hear small fragments from where I am, '…you were always hard-headed…', 'No, that was twenty-three years ago, you are getting old and muddle-headed!' Their voices are deep and comforting. They have known each other a long time, you can hear the familiarity in their voices, see it in the way their bodies move.

'Another street has been closed off and is gone. Can you believe they are even demolishing streets?' my father says.

Sun's father grunts. 'Aiya! Which street?'

'Beijing West, where we used to sit with the birds…' They talk of the past each time they sit together like it is the present, a never-ending present. I can almost see the small cane birdcages they would take out.

My mother is frying vegetables. The wok is angry with fire. Flames dart up around her but her face is not the same strong edifice it was. The glare of the flames highlights her frailty even more. I grab the wok from her and she grunts and moves back to a chopping board. I'm happy to lift one of her burdens. The food smells fresh, looks vibrant.

Sun comes by me, kisses the back of my neck and I smile. We make eye contact briefly as he says, 'Home late. You should rest more.' His eyes are happy, bright. I nod and focus on the vegetables.

He puts a bottle of very expensive foreign red wine on the bench, says, 'Let's celebrate.'

I turn, kiss his lips softly but he's too excited to respond to my lips. He says, 'I signed that big new contract I've told you about.'

'Oh.' I nod, I am still puzzled by the lack of detail. I ask him what the new job entails but he lets my question disappear. Did he hear me? Is he really listening?

He continues, 'It will launch us into the sky, Zhen. It's a very big deal, we need to drink!' He pours glasses of wine hastily and spills trails of red liquid on the bench. I drink first. He gives glasses to our fathers as I sip it. It is smooth, warm.

'You want children soon?' Sun's father yells at me. Sun and I realise they are all looking at us, watching us. My cheeks burn, and I shout above the wok, 'It's expensive now. But you'll get your grandchild.' My father grunts, stares at his tiles, as if his future is there.

Sun's father smiles at me, mouth wide open. I can see his gold teeth catch the dim light.

I finish chopping for my mother. She dumps the vegetables into the pan with some egg and starts to fry, her teeth tight together. Lost in her own thoughts. I wonder if it's the note but I don't want to be the one to start something so I don't ask. I get some tofu for her from the fridge, ready to chop.

'Throw that away. It's rubbish,' my mother says.

'It looks good to me.'

'The company have been caught adding brake fluid to their tofu. They deserve to be shot. A bullet in the head is too good.'

I grip her shoulders and squeeze her briefly. This normally makes her frown, but she doesn't react this time, she just moves and tosses vegetables across the wok, her eyes reflecting the flames.

'You been drinking the cooking wine?' I ask, and laugh at my own joke. She grunts like my father, tells me not to 'waste all the hot wind' inside me.

My father calls out, 'You are lucky to live now, so lucky. You have it easy…' One of the usual rambles we get while they play mah-jong. We are 'weak with too many choices, too soft'. These rambling rivers of words flow with the alcohol. I love my father, but he thinks all we need is a full belly and a roof over our heads to be happy. What about all the other details? We need money to eat and a house to keep warm, but we need more for happiness. Where does the heart fit into his world?

Sun tells his father to 'move his hands, not his mouth' and nods at the tiles. His father points at him. 'You are too smart, too much education.' Perhaps there is too much time between our generations; words can't bridge some distances. Food arrives at the table. My mother takes the note and throws it onto the mah-jong tiles and the two fathers look at her.

Breaking the uneasy silence that follows, I say, 'Not long now, no more mud.' I smile at my mum, but her face hardens. I feel like I'm playing the peacemaker again. Stretched like a membrane between them.

Sun's dad coughs a little, starts turning his glass around in his hand nervously; we've had this talk before. He says, 'You will get somewhere new, warm, big windows over the city. Very good!'

My father grits his teeth, 'I want to stay here, but not in a high-rise.' My mother shoots him a short sharp stare. She can see where this is going. I try to change the topic, talk about the thick snow we got last night.

Sun, who normally avoids these exchanges, pulls something out of his pocket. 'Look I have a brochure of your new place...' I feel my stomach tighten. '... It's in the north part of the city, on the twenty-third floor with views back over the mountains.'

My father starts to dig into the rice in the middle of the table. There is another long pause and I feel a shiver down my spine. He shifts back in his chair to speak.

'We will be like pigeons in a cage up there.'

'It can work in your favour. You can rent out the place they give you when this is demolished, and move to this much better place. You'll be a land-lord!' Sun pushes on.

My father smirks. 'You sound like an investment person from the bank, not a son-in-law.'

Sun laughs. 'That's what lots of people do. They are very happy.'

I start to eat. My mother, who rarely drinks, pours herself a cup of wine. She holds her gaze on my fiancé for a few moments. My father stares into his drink. I watch Sun, puzzled why he has weighed into this. I see a change in him, but I can't quite find words to identify it.

Sun's dad says, 'When you see the new place... What a view! I'll be jealous of you, old man; your place will be better than—'

'It will be a cage for an old man.' My father groans. Sun steps to the other side of Father now, cornering him in his chair.

My mother stands frozen, hovering. She glares at him, a cold hard stare willing him to keep his lips together. But no one can command my father, he has his own mind. 'To make it worse they are rushing this through, illegally.' Sun looks up at me to say something but I've had enough. I jam my lips shut. I now see them pushing him into a corner. I don't like to watch this.

Sun smiles and says, 'I know how you feel, it's a common feeling...'

My mother breaks in. 'Just accept the money, you old fool! We can go somewhere else with that amount of money, but you—' I try to stop my mother. My father has gone red, looks at the table. 'No, let me finish,' she says. 'You can have your own little house for that out of town. I just want to go. I hate living like this, in this shithole. How much of this do you think I can handle? Hmm?'

Sun's dad has left the room. Sun stands back, can only look at me, his eyes urging me again to say something but I don't know what to say. Have those dirty numbers started this open warfare tonight?

My mother grabs the note, waves it in my father's face. 'How can you say no to this? For once in our life we get some luck, and you want to say no? This is good money.'

Sun talks about money and real estate prices to blast my father with options. He is intense about it, almost aggressive. I'm angry that Sun has muddied the waters even more. My mother nods, hand on her hip now, head bobbing. She stands over my father. He is being attacked by numbers. Is this what our family has become? Have they been bought by a few figures?

For the first time, I feel sorry for my father. I don't want him attacked over money. I can't keep quiet now. 'Maybe he has his own point of view. Maybe we should leave him...'

'My home,' my mother says at the top of her voice, 'is not a civil war battlefield. Eat and be quiet, all of you!' I grab the note and push it into my pocket so we don't have to look at it as we eat. Sun frowns. My mother slams the aubergine down and some of the food spills out onto the table. Sauce oozes towards the mah-jong tiles.

It's the most silent meal we have ever eaten. Sun motions to me with his head as I finish. He leaves the table silently for the bedroom and I follow. I can only hear the soft clicking of my parents' chopsticks as they stare into their rice. Sun's father has left the house without even saying goodbye. I feel horrible, empty. A fish whose guts have been left to spill out after the knife has entered. I wish I could take back my outburst but it spilt out like water. Too late.

Sun's voice is hoarse, quiet, menacing. 'You embarrassed me. I was only trying to help your father; he needs the advice. We had almost convinced him!' He points.

I grab his finger. 'Couldn't you see he didn't want any more pressure?' I stare at him as we lock eyes.

He pokes my chest. 'You should support me. No one wants to keep living like this.'

I feel blood rush to my chest. I want to strike him but I don't. 'I know! Why are you so passionate about this property mess now?'

He speaks over me. 'No one can stop the building, and he's an old man. He'll be better off when they move.'

'This is still his home. He needs time to be ready.'

Sun wets his lips, pauses. 'It's you that wanted to be out of here quickly, you who talked about central air con and a bigger place.'

'I still want that!' I pick up my packed bags from next to me to demonstrate my point. The click of my parents' chopsticks in the room behind me makes me even angrier at Sun. I throw the two bags at his legs and he falls back against the wall. I do this without thinking. It's a sort of anger I haven't felt before. Sun gets up and turns to go, grabs his bag. He turns to leave the house.

'Where are you going?' I snap, no longer whispering. I hear the sound of chopsticks halt behind me. He stops with his back to me but doesn't reply. I reach out to grab him, but he moves as I do and he's gone. My feet remain frozen, numb, and I don't stop him.

I think about what Sun Tzu says about being 'acquainted with their designs'.

For the first time I don't know what Sun's designs are.

*

Lindon

When I come back to the hotel each evening any trace of me has been cleansed; guests are messy blots on pure space, blowflies on white sheets. There aren't even any sounds I would register as being homely; only the buzz of air con and the distant thud of other hotel doors.

I leave the room as I do every morning, but this morning I put a 'Do not disturb' card on the handle and mess up the soaps and throw my clothes on the floor. A hotel is just a crack between stones in the road, we aren't supposed to really live in them; but I want to go back and see traces of me in the room today.

My taxi gets caught in the tail of a giant snake of humanity trying to slither onto one of the elevated freeways that pull traffic away from the suffocated streets below. I gaze out into the thick haze trying to spot landmarks I have learnt to recognise, but the features of the city are hidden behind a blind of grey and the traffic grinds to a halt.

I close my eyes, trying to understand the pit in my stomach, the feeling I am sinking into myself. I wonder if I am homesick, oversaturated with the greys of the city I find myself lost in, compass smashed. I try and imagine the house I shared with Julie in Australia; I see light spilling through the widows, the table by the front door cluttered with keys and mail but I can't see Julie in the house. I am wandering through memories of an empty shell and when I open my eyes I find the concrete more comforting than those sun-faded images.

Our site office is an old shipping container with one cheap, ill-fitting window carved out of the side containing an air conditioner that drives against the cold, vibrating the window slightly in its frame. The only thing that marks my presence in this place is a small postcard from Sydney I have jammed under the window frame at a jarring angle.

The translator checks his hair in the reflection of the window. A small crack runs up from the corner of the pane of glass and fans out into fractured glass twigs where his eyes reflect back off the surface. I slump in a chair and stare at the gaps in the window – how does China work if it doesn't all quite fit together, if the air whistles through the gaps?

I have a vague sense of once thinking I had a home. We use the word glibly, the way we talk about a heartbeat or a breath we take in but I didn't have that feeling with Julie – we lived in a house, a frame cloaked in glass and plaster that pretended to be some sort of home. What made those cheap, crappy old draughty weatherboard places I froze and sweated in as a kid feel like an actual 'home'?

I turn to the translator, on a whim. 'Find me a place I can walk to the office from, a real place to live.'

I don't think he really gets what I mean. He just stares at me and finishes smoothing down hair that looked perfect to begin with, so I raise my voice slightly; frustration gnaws at me. 'Find me an apartment to live in.'

He frowns. 'But the hotel, it's one of the best.'

I have no patience this morning, I talk over the top of his chatter. 'Give me some options this morning.'

He shrugs and says there will be an agent still open across the road that he can call. He gets up and wanders down the end of the container with his

47

phone, starts a call, and I stare out of the window to try and tune his voice out of my head. It's still outside, like the grey and the ice have frozen the blood that pumps around the site. Cranes are motionless, generators are off and the workers' compound in the distance is locked and empty. The Spring Festival will grip the entire country soon: as many as thirty million people have now started to go home to celebrate with their families.

Foreigners are out of sync with all this, dislocated – maybe that explains how I feel this morning.

As the translator speaks on his phone I twist my head and stare at the nail house. I imagine cutting the power lines to the house, as he continues to flood the container with his words; imagine watching the house light flicker out, see them run outside into the snow. It makes me feel many different things.

When he finishes his call I ask the translator, 'How long could you live in a house without power or water at this time of year?' I nod in the direction of the nail house.

'Here is the number you need to call for the apartment. I'd suggest you call now, before everyone is gone for the festival.' Cold air bursts in as he opens the door to leave and my question remains hanging in the chilled air, unanswered, sharp and dangerous.

Dialling the number later, I'm irritated to hear Zhen's voice. After a long pause I say, 'I have called the real estate agency, haven't I?'

There is silence at her end as well. I think I hear an intake of breath. 'Yes... you have dialled the right number.'

I unravel my plans to her. To my great relief she says, 'I am busy. I will send someone else in an hour or so. Is that too soon?'

She hangs up on me before I can reply. I smile out into the haze. I wander for an hour, watch people coming and going. I stop for a while and eat sweet potato cooked in a large drum of smouldering coal. The potato is warm, comforting. Sleet has started to descend in sheets through the grey and it melts in small buds of water as it hits my coat. I pull my scarf tightly round my neck and carefully make my way towards the entrance when the hour is up, trying not to slip on the ice, the figure I need to meet drowning in dirty sky. I walk towards him, a wind picks up and I hear a metallic grinding from somewhere above me and I stop, look up, squint into the gloom.

Another gust and it's as if some huge metal creature above me is shifting its weight, stretching – a giant Chinese dragon of some kind. The wind goes down and the sound slips through the sleet, settles.

I walk towards the figure, whose back is towards me. I get a couple of paces away and I look over my shoulder, expecting to see someone but there is no one and I turn round in time to see the figure facing me. I feel my guts tighten and something flood around my blood – it's Zhen.

'I thought you were sending someone else?'

She looks irritated, stamps a bit in the cold. 'Yes. She had some personal troubles. I had to come instead.' Her voice trails off and she turns and walks away. I follow. Sleet buries our footsteps, cleanses them.

Neither of us talk; it's too cold anyway. I focus on the back of her large black overcoat as we trudge up the street away from the site.

We seem to stop our stride abruptly just as we were starting to get going; she is staring up at a block of flats that are still standing at the back of the site, flats that are supposed to be demolished. We are at a back entrance I didn't know about – that doesn't appear on the plans.

'It's not pretty. But it's very cheap and you said you wanted to be close.' Plumes of steam come out of her mouth as she says this.

Paint peels off in chaotic patches, small cracks run through the surface layer of cement and there is an all-pervading smell of dampness that seems to ooze from the building.

The lift shudders up to the flat we are going to see; it feels like it's about to stall halfway up. The light barely works in here and it smells like the steel itself has been devoured slowly from the inside. How could anybody want to live in this dump if they knew they could move into a new apartment?

We get to the fifth floor, the top floor, and she rattles the key in the lock for a minute or so. Dust falls on her as she tries to get it to budge. She stops and frowns at me midway through, says it must be 'a lazy lock' and goes on attacking it. We hear a small crunch as the lock mechanism seems to give up, and we move inside.

Zhen goes straight for the window to let some air in. It's clear no one has been in here for weeks, maybe more, and the window casement is jammed. The cupboard doors look scratched and old; two don't have any handles any more. Mould has started to make patterns on the ceilings; the smell of it is overpowering.

This must be a joke, a taunt from Zhen Yi – she wants me to leave enraged, disappointed. I feel my throat becoming dry, irritated by every gasp of mould I inhale. I turn from her, compose myself. When we do make eye contact a smile spreads across my face, but it's a constructed smile.

Zhen moves back towards the front door and reaches for the handle. She stops before she tries it. Without looking away from the door, says to me, 'Let my office know what you think.' She then starts to pull down on the handle and I turn away towards the window. From where I am I can just see a hazy sky and the side of a crane.

Zhen pulls quickly three times on the handle and I hear a small crack. 'Shit!' She is standing dumbfounded with the handle in her hand. I move towards her to help and she gives it to me. I attempt to re-attach it but it's rusted and the mechanism is broken right through. She moves away from me towards the window and rust flakes off in my hands, stains my skin red.

I put the handle on the kitchen bench and return slowly to the window. It's as if the haze outside is inside me today. I feel like I'm sinking. Zhen is on the phone, speaking in Chinese in a raised voice. I assume she is asking someone to come and get us out. I stand beside her and look down. Shoulder to shoulder with Zhen, I can smell a fragrance from her, flowery, sweet. It blocks out the stench of mould. I see her face tense, pensive as I look across at her. Looking into my eyes for the first time, she says, 'It might be a while… The locksmith is busy.'

'I can pay the locksmith if it helps, least I can do.'

She checks her phone as she says, 'Yes, everything is fixed with money.'

I rub the windowpane in front of me. 'Well, when it is a question of cash, then it can help.'

She snorts. 'Everything has a price, doesn't it? Is that how life is for you?'

My fingertips are stained from the glass, I try and rub the grime off on the frame. 'Of course not everything.'

'You think an extra zero or two will change someone's mind on an important decision? We all have a price?'

I turn, smile. 'Well, it would change my mind.'

She looks me in the eye. 'Typical. Now I know you.'

I fold my arms, sigh. She has made her mind up about me and it's a version of me I don't recognise.

I raise my voice. 'I'm not just a cardboard cut-out, a "type".'

She arches her eyebrows and her lips move as if she wants to say something but no sound comes out. I press on. 'I won't win a prize for thinking this relates to me sticking my neck out to get your family a better deal. Is that it? I'm a demon for trying to give you something more?'

She looks back out of the window. She is so close to the glass as she speaks, it clouds the view. 'You have put me into the eye of a storm. I'm in between two warring camps.' Her voice is fragile, shows cracks spreading out in all directions.

There is a pause. I feel myself cooling down, wishing I could change what I have just said. I reach out and touch her arm. 'I'm sorry...' I begin, 'but you must understand...' My voice peters out.

She mutters, 'No, it's OK.'

There is more silence between us. I feel like I have sunk so far now I don't know how to climb back up. I squint into the haze, trying to see through it, but I'm blind. 'It's not that easy for me to see what's going on...' I don't know why I say what tumbles out next; are there some people whose eyes are keys that unlock things inside us? It seems natural to say it. 'I'm actually homesick, lost. I have no idea what the fuck I'm doing.'

She looks at me again, sighs. 'I don't...'

'You don't have to apologise.'

She smirks. 'I wasn't going to. I was just going to say I don't know what the fuck I'm doing either.'

A gust of wind has cleared the sky and from here I can see the site spread out below me clearly now, laid out like a giant three-dimensional model.

She says, half to herself, 'This place stinks.' She brings a hand up and cups it over her nose.

I put my phone on the windowsill, reach out and tug at the window to open it. I pull as hard as I can but it feels welded into place. I put so much force into it my hand slips and crashes against the pane of glass. I hear a crack, then the sound of breaking glass and the high pitch of wind whistling into the holes.

Zhen looks startled and grabs my arm, pulling me back away from the window to see if I'm OK. The glass has cut small holes in my jacket. She helps me pull it off, and we examine my arm. Her fingers run over my skin, and she pushes open my hand looking for wounds. I recoil as she finishes. No blood, no wound.

She says, 'Do you always open windows like that?'

'I don't think I could afford it.'

We look at each other for a moment, and then a small smile creeps across her face. I look back out of the window. I see her father, a tiny harmless miniature now, shovelling ice and snow away from his doorway. At the edge of that pit he looks like he is standing on the edge of the world. The light from his house is the only warmth from the site, a tiny home clinging to an earthy precipice.

Zhen turns to me and looks back into the room we are in. 'It has character...' Her lip quivers, has the potential of a smile again.

I pull my focus back to the room, look around again. 'It has something,' I reply. We both look at the place seriously for the first time.

'It's actually pretty bad, isn't it?' Zhen says.

'Well, the view is good.' I begin to feel guilty about my question to the translator early in the morning. I am thawing out despite the cold.

'I think I brought you here as punishment.'

Twisting back to the view, I say, 'I wanted some-where close to work, and I can see everything from here. It's what I want.' What's left of the glass in front of us fogs up with our breath and the cranes are hidden.

Zhen hunches over and peers through the hole I made. 'I can see the executive pool here, and the golf course just over there.' She laughs as we gaze down at the scar of mud and snow underneath.

I look around the place again, then back out of the window. I say, 'I guess you have yourself a deal, but—'

I hear a voice yell, '*Ni hao*' from the corridor and Zhen yells back, moves to the door. They have a quick conversation in Chinese and there is the sound of tools in the lock, the door straining. A short time later dust flies up into the air in small plumes as the door explodes open. Two workmen peer in at us, burst our moment, intrude. I almost feel disappointed.

Zhen turns as she is about to slip out of the room. 'Yes, I will have a team of people come and scrub this place and, if you are lucky, maybe give it a coat of paint.' She waves goodbye.

Later when I go back to my hotel I unlock the door. They have ignored my 'Do not disturb' sign and all traces of me have been obliterated once more. There is a mint on my pillow. I sigh, get ready for bed and lie on top of the perfectly pressed blanket. The answer to my question about what a home is comes to me as I drift off to sleep, alone on my pristine queen-sized bed. I forget about the mint and it smears into my hair as I sleep.

III

Zhen

We are all dressed to stay out late. I can smell
perfume even over the food. I feel light and excited
in the city. No family on my shoulders, no mud. I
can forget about the foreigner, broken panes of glass
and large numbers.

The sounds of friends chattering are one of life's
sweet melodies, a melody best heard over food. We
always need full stomachs before we go drinking.

'My parents think any man who marries me now
has to have a car. They watch too much Shanghai
TV,' my friend Na says.

Steam rises between us. I picture my father
still struggling with the door as I left, its top hinge
coming loose. Him with his rusty tools perched
up on a stool. The house is always threatening to
finish falling down at any moment. My mother,
behind, is withdrawn, sedated by television.

Na throws a spoonful of quail eggs into the bubbling pot in front of us, laughs, rolls her eyes. Mei says, 'Cars are good. Convenient. Your parents aren't as dumb as you.' Na pokes out her tongue and Mei shrugs. Mei has had her hair done again. It is streaked red and she has painted her fingernails a matching colour.

Lele, a small girl with big smiling eyes, doesn't say much. She is shovelling noodles into her mouth and watching people stream past the window outside. She breaks her silence. 'You have to find a man who doesn't wear brand names; it shows they have too much money and will discard you like an old shirt.'

Na scoffs. 'If he discards you and he is rich, at least he might have bought you an apartment!'

I point at Na. 'As Sun Tzu says, if he does stay around "he is relying on the natural strength of his position" to get you.'

Mei laughs so loudly people look over at us. 'She's quoting Sun Tzu, *shu daizi*!'

I feel my face go warm with embarrassment. No one reads Sun Tzu any more; she has called me a 'bookworm'. I am different from them, strange.

I glance up at the TV attached to the wall above us, disengaging from this conversation. Mei thinks I have got lucky with Sun. Despite him not having a car. My mother and father are happy because Sun is of the same 'level' as us. Same class.

Well educated with a good income that will only get larger. They say 'love fades but a marriage is about getting someone who can take care of you'.

The news comes on the TV, a local channel. I can't hear the newsreader over the hum of the restaurant. Mei elbows me: 'So?' I'm startled; I didn't even know she'd asked me anything. She says, 'We want the gossip on you and Sun. How did you get such a good catch?'

I start chewing again so I can't reply. I keep my eyes on the TV to evade any more part in the conversation.

Lele says, 'You don't eat very much, maybe he thought you were cheap.'

I elbow Lele, but before I can fire back at her with a smart comment I see myself on TV. I'm arguing with Lindon. Our dog is running towards him and he is leaning forwards trying to be powerful but he is using his hands like a big child. He looks unsteady, undignified. I feel my cheeks glow, notice I have stopped eating. It sounds like a blanket has been thrown over the restaurant noise.

Na looks up. She starts choking on her noodles as she laughs and chews at the same time. Small droplets of soup spray out of her mouth and she shields her face with her hand. 'Zhen is a TV star now!'

Lele squeals, 'Arguing with a handsome foreigner too!'

I shove Lele again. It was supposed to be the gesture of a friend but she recoils and I realise I have hit her too hard. She glares at me, so I say, 'It's my father's shitty business, not mine. And who said he is handsome?' But when I glance back up at Lindon, the dog locked onto his ankle, there is something charming about him. His directness was a display of desperation, weakness. I felt the urge to protect him and I feel more sorry for him seeing this again.

I try and draw people's focus away from the TV. A young couple at the table next to us are looking from the TV to me and back again and talking in hushed tones. I say to Lele, 'Sun is lucky to have me, isn't he? He will be marrying a TV personality.' They think I'm 'shameless', and there is lots of laughter. I don't look at the TV again, but I am thinking about Lindon.

'Life is not a romantic TV show or a love song,' Mei says, like she has given up on all the poetry, 'it's an investment.'

We finish the hot pot. There's nothing left to pick out. Na asks if I'm still coming out with them. I don't want to go home; I want to stay with them. I want to laugh. I want to stay in our world, forget.

We argue about who will pay the bill. I race from the table to the counter first, beating Lele. She uses her height to thrust a wad of notes at the waiter first. We check phones, catch our reflections in glass and pretend we aren't checking our hair. We shuffle out between tables and head to the door.

My phone buzzes. Mei has come over to us and grabs it from me. She's trying to intercept my messages. It's a call, I realise in horror, from my father. I grab the phone back and walk away from them. My father is breathless; I can hear the sound of trolleys and noise in the background. 'Your mother has had a turn. In hospital. Meet us there.'

He hangs up. I feel my heart race and I walk quickly out to the street to find a taxi.

On the way to the hospital I tick off all the good qualities about Sun, try to remind myself how exciting buying the flat will be. Remind myself how lucky I am. I picture the 'double happiness' paper cut-outs up on my door.

*

Lindon

It only took the workers Zhen hired a few days to get the place liveable – the smell of fresh paint from my new apartment is stuck in my nose from my first night there. I would rather still be there settling in and unpacking but here I am, stuffing more small delicate cold dishes down my gullet again. Banquets were once an exotic adventure to email home about, but now they are tedious, slow. I can't taste anything.

An assorted group of project people are here as a thank you for our work with them so far, developing what the translator described to me as 'the relationships for doing business'. There are no transactions here in China of any kind that are somehow free of the relationships that drive them and I wonder now how cold we are with each other back home – how easy it is to forget the *people* you are doing the business with. Here today there are local government guys, the health inspection team, the safety inspector, and people who are just described as 'contracting representatives'. When introduced to me they harden their smiles, don't bother to say much. I have been in the country long enough now to read smiles and some body language; I have become literate. I understand from all this that I'm just the token white face, the outsider. But I won't be here long enough to be worth gaining their understanding and recognition. I catch myself feeling a small twinge of melancholy at this, but push the feeling away. This is just business for me, I remind myself.

One guy doesn't smile at all, doesn't even bother to go through the motions with me. I ask quietly who he is. The translator says he is in the propaganda department. I say, 'Propaganda?'

'Sorry, Marketing.' We both smile. It's a smile with no heart in it. They continue 'building relationships'. I watch, the eternal spectator.

I have drunk too much; again, I'm starting to feel the effects unsettling my stomach. I try to ask questions about the nail house and the only thing I get is laughter. 'Stupid nail house…' someone says to me. He introduces himself as Frank; I have seen him before in our company offices. His face is bright red in reaction to the alcohol and he glows under the lights.

We are drinking a pungent-smelling white spirit that costs hundreds of people's currency dollars per bottle. It burns away their talk of work. The translator loosens up a little after three bowls of the spirit. I ask him if he has family, trying to be polite, and he says he has 'a very demanding wife in the city, and a friend outside'. I ask what he means by friend and he says, 'My weekend lady…' He trails off, looks into his cup. The waitress notices and tops it up.

A succession of hot dishes and soups come and go. My thought patterns slow and frustration turns to dull irritation. The translator must be able to read me and he says, 'The business in China is the *eating* and *drinking*, not the other way around.'

Double Happiness cigarettes are being placed by everyone's bowls, interrupting us as we finish eating. I notice wallpaper is peeling off the walls. I feel queasy now so I stop drinking anything and put my hand over my cup as a waitress tries to pour me more spirit.

Everyone starts rising, a signal the meal is over. Guests stuff the cigarette packets into their jackets and head to the door in clouds of smoke. I'm relieved. Everyone moves quickly out of the room, the crowd begins to evaporate, but two of our official guests stay and talk. I follow everyone else down a dim passage with faded reproduction prints of Chinese paintings in cracked frames, towards the front door. As we get close, the light from outside is luminous, blinding.

I am close to the light when I realise I have left my scarf on the back of a chair and I double back towards the room. I dodge a waitress carrying a bowl of steaming crab. The door to our room is still open and I can see, from the corridor where I stop, Frank standing with someone. I don't recognise the person at first; I strain closer to see, and then I realise it's the safety inspector. Frank pushes him a large brown office envelope. It has so much cash in it the corners of the banknotes stick out from the end of the package. I feel a wave of nausea from the alcohol wash over me and I steady myself against a door on my left to another banquet room. It's loud behind me. I hear many voices but I struggle against the waves washing through my head and keep fixed on these two figures.

I see the translator go back into our banquet room from a back door; he interrupts the deal but doesn't seem to see what's going on. The package disappears into the safety inspector's coat and, with timid jittery glances, the two men begin to exit the room quickly. The translator walks past them without looking up, his eyes on his phone.

Afraid of being seen as they leave, I step backwards into the room to my left and out of the corridor. I feel almost overwhelmed by alcohol and move unsteadily, off balance. The translator exits the banquet room before the two men. He must have seen me and follows me into the other room closing the door behind himself.

Someone is pushing something into my back. I turn round, startled. Behind me, the room is full of people seated at tables. A big red 'double happiness' decoration hangs over a table with what looks like a bride and groom sitting at it, grinning from ear to ear at me. Most of the room is looking at me now.

The groom, who has pushed a large bowl of white wine towards me, says to me in English, 'Welcome! Cheers!' He makes me take the bowl and many people start to raise a toast, eyes on me. I feel compelled to play along.

I smile and say, 'Cheers, congratulations,' and they watch as I'm embarrassed into drinking even more wine. I finish, wipe away the leftover from my mouth, the room spins and, to everyone's horror, I throw up at the feet of the bride and groom. I'm so sick I can't follow Frank and I wonder where he has gone. I apologise as best I can but I'm having trouble stringing words together. The newlyweds just stare at me, horrified. The translator does his best to smooth things over as we back out of the room. He pulls the Double Happiness cigarettes out of my jacket and hands the packet to the groom.

The old wallpaper is spinning as we leave. I close my eyes and see hundred-dollar bills floating around underneath my eyelids and I can't make them go away. Can money buy everything?

The translator makes me drink a two-litre bottle of water in the taxi. The air con in the car is broken and the iciness of the air and all that water bring me back to life. The translator thinks I should go home but I insist over his protests that I have work to do on-site. I shiver as we pull up beside the row of blue steel fencing.

I unfold myself from the taxi, ignoring the way the ground seems to tilt underneath my feet. It has snowed again, a light icing of white, which makes me struggle even more to trudge forwards. As I shuffle through the gate, my head like wood being split with an axe, I hear footsteps crunching in the snow behind me; it is the translator. He puts an arm round me and steadies me, and I feel the ground firm beneath me. I turn to him but his face is too close and blurry. The words are difficult to get out, 'How long have you... how long have you been married?'

He kicks some debris away from our feet. 'Five years. We met at University.'

I grimace. 'Romance doesn't last, gets ripped from you... taken away...'

The translator sighs. 'Yes, Mr Lindon, I am sure.'

'How can it happen...? How can someone fuck someone else? How can you throw it all away?' I feel nausea crash over me and I am not sure if it's that dragging the betrayal out of a dark corner of my head or the alcohol. I go on, words tumbling out into the cold air. 'Don't trust anyone, you can't... ripped away, all fucked up. Now look at me, look where I am?'

The translator stops. I don't know if it's to catch his breath or something I have said. My head spins. Without him I would be in the snow. He says, 'You are here now, Mr Lindon, this is yours.' He looks out over the site, nods at me. 'Every end has something new after it.'

I start to laugh; my body shudders with it. 'What corny shit...' and I feel the contents of my stomach rise and I am sick in the snow. The translator doesn't let go, but holds me and keeps me on my feet.

When I raise my head I can see, in the distance, someone leaving Zhen's family home, suitcases in their hands. I think it might be Zhen.

*

Zhen

The hospital is overrun; the doctors seem to be struggling to get everyone seen. We watch patients queue outside my mother's room back up the corridor. Our doctor still hasn't come.

My mother chews on nuts we have brought, says the food is terrible. I offer to get her dinner tonight. Sun says I should stay with my family; he smiles and disappears to 'make arrangements' for her. He has taken charge. Mother gripes about the food and her companion in the room, peels fruit and watches us.

The companion says, 'The food will kill us first!' and they chat for a while. She says my mum has a 'good daughter' and points at me. Her plastic hospital bracelet hangs down; her wrist is thin, shrunken. I say I'm just 'OK', show my modesty, as I should. My mother says I work too hard but there's something of a look of approval about this. It fades when my father comes in. The petals fall off her face, drop to the floor.

'Sun's gone to get food. Some more blankets too.'

My father sniffs, throws two newspapers down beside Mum. She grabs one without making eye contact with him. The property drama is erecting concrete walls between them. I start peeling nuts, and spit husks into old newspaper.

'You should be getting it, not Sun,' I say to him. He must feel my hurt, my anger. I hold him responsible for my mother being here, for her getting this sick, this tired. He looks down, avoids my eyes.

My mother says, suddenly, 'Nothing is forever.' I almost choke on a nut. I can't stop her; she continues, 'You are here on earth, and then you aren't.'

I grab a cup of water my mum has beside her, drink it so quickly it runs down my chin. I can feel it fan out under my shirt. I hear my father slip out behind me. He knows when to go.

'Aiya!' I say. 'You're sick, tired, stop talking like that!' I drink some more water. 'You sound like a strange old TV series.' The anger I felt towards her and Sun at home is gone. It's been replaced by shock at her strange talk.

She puts down her newspaper. 'Well; that's it, ignore it if you want to but that's life.' She looks through me like she is talking to ghosts. My mother never talks like this. There's never any reference to mortality in our house. Not even a footnote.

I grab her hand, squeeze it. 'Don't talk shit, you will be here forever, nagging me.' She is silent, stares out of the window.

I don't want to know she will really die one day. Life is hard enough. I need someone to hold; I want

Sun now. He does come a moment later and I jump up but stop myself from touching him, stand but don't reach out to him. He frowns at me, doesn't pull me close either.

Mother says to Sun, 'I've been rambling like an old lady to her.' Sun smiles, of course, tells her he's sure it's not rambling. I poke my tongue out at her and go and get some more water.

I force my way through the queue, which seems to have travelled a little towards the consultation rooms and away from my mother's room. A giant crack runs up the wall from behind the water cooler to the ceiling. Moths buzz around the lights above; one bulb flickers. I drink the water, lean against the wall; wonder how long it will take for the crack to slowly work its way through the whole building. Do we fall apart starting with one small crack?

When I come back in Sun is messaging someone – he smiles at the screen. He doesn't know I've come into the room. I slip in quietly, stand behind him. I crane slightly on tiptoes to look over him to see his phone, but as I do Sun realises and he recoils slightly. He shields the screen from me, pulls it towards his stomach. I ask him who it was and he says it's a funny anecdote about a client. I ask him for details and he seems to hesitate too much. Like he's making things up.

I shrug; move over to a chair while he stands. The lady in the bed next to my mother points at Sun, asks, 'How much do you earn?' Sun has a figure he always gives in this situation, a fake amount. He adds to it each year for inflation. He tells her the figure; she nods in approval, says, 'Not bad.' She goes back to her nuts.

Sun gets another message. I watch him and he knows I'm watching. He doesn't read it straight away. He delays, pretends to be concerned by the blankets. Buttons up his jacket. It is getting cold in this room. I can see steam coming out of my mouth now. Has the heating gone off again? He eventually looks at the screen; I watch his eyes follow the lines across it, absorbing it. I get up quickly, flushed, driven. I reach him and ask him to show me. Make up some shit about wanting to see what goes on at his work.

'Boring, probably much like your work messages.' He hands over his phone but drags his thumb across the screen. The last message is gone, deleted. I turn to him to say something, to start asking questions. But he is saved by the arrival of the doctor.

Is Sun having an affair? Has he been caught on the end of a line by a girl with make-up and designer bags? I dismiss the idea as quickly as it floats into my head. A silly thought at the end of a stressful night. But it doesn't completely go away. It stays there, that idea. It stays just on the edges of my thoughts, unnerves me. I resent his smile, his endless charm. What's real?

The doctor says my mother is exhausted, needs rest and peace. I walk out of the hospital room as she finishes. It feels like the ground is moving beneath me. I want things to settle. Sun follows me but I tell him I'm going home alone. He stops as I get to the lift.

I go to my parents'. I march straight into my room and grab my bags, fumble with a rucksack and haul it over my shoulder. I will go to Mei's tonight and have some fun. I can't be here any more. I tell myself it's just the need to stay with a friend, but I can't escape my frustration with Sun, my unease. I leave quickly in case I run into him. If I don't see him I can explain via a casual text message.

Instead, I see Lindon on the way out with his translator. He is unsteady on his feet. As I get closer it's clear he has been drinking again. Perhaps that's what foreigners do. I wonder if he has been in a fight, fucked a girl. I feel a strange needle of pain with this last thought.

How ridiculous. I get close to him, stop. My cases crunch in the ice as they drop. My fingers ache. I can smell the alcohol on him. I tell him how potent Chinese wines are.

Lindon looks like a crushed flower on ice as he sways in front of me. He is lost and breaking apart. His eyes seem to see through me.

I suddenly don't want to pick up the cases again. I was running away. Will this help me? Lindon staggers and falls towards me. I am so shocked as his body falls into my arms that I don't hold him, but let him slip from me and fall to the ground. His face strikes the ice and stains it with blood.

His translator helps me drag him back to my parents' house. My house. It's then I tell myself I need to help Lindon. He is the key to getting my mother the peace she needs. I ask the translator to drag in my cases as I pour vinegar on the small scratches in Lindon's face. I hold his head in my hands. Tectonic plates are moving everything.

*

Lindon

I am on Zhen's father's old plastic-covered sofa, wincing as the vinegar Zhen is using to clean my wounds stings the flesh. My face flushes with each touch of her fingers on my skin; it makes the sting feel distant, far away.

Her words aren't barbed today. She looks out of the window in between dabs. 'I've lived here most of my life.' I watch the light catch on the edge of her lips and notice how it plays around them. She continues, 'They used to call it "Revolutionary Hero Area", or something like that. It was for political cadres. That was a long time ago.'

'Your father was a revolutionary?' She has lost the look of an enemy.

She puts down the small vinegar-soaked cloth and looks at me. 'No, my mother was. My father argued with people, learnt English from textbooks when the schools were closed in the sixties. It was my mother who was out fighting. Fighting for the country,' she says.

I touch my wounded cheek. 'Your dad is the fighter now.'

Zhen smiles and picks the cloth back up. 'He fights for tumbling-down hovels. My mother fought bigger fights. Fights for things you can't touch with your hands. Ideals.'

I sit up, look out of the window at the falling snow. 'Your dad can understand English?'

'He has forgotten a lot. He still remembers many of the yellow words.'

'What are "yellow" words?'

'Shit, fuck…' She starts to laugh now. Taken off guard, I forget my aching head, and laughter spills from me as well. She adds between giggles, 'Sorry… They are "yellow" words; I guess you would say "rude" words? I don't know, it's your language.'

'I'm crap at languages…' I notice the snow has started to thin. It has dusted the ground with a delicate fresh layer. The scarred mud is covered – the building site outside seems soft in the dwindling light of sunset. 'I'm struggling to even get the basics of Chinese right. Your father puts me to shame, even just remembering the dirty bits.'

She leans forwards and dabs my cheek with the cloth. She is so close I can smell her hair, her skin. She says, 'Understanding people is harder than understanding words.'

'We can agree on that.'

There is silence for a while. Zhen rubs more vinegar into my face and winces as I wince. I can't remember the last time someone has shown such care about me. Has it been years? When did these moments dry up in my marriage? Zhen pushes a little too hard into my cheek, a bolt of pain makes me pull my head back suddenly and I reach out for her hand and grab it, pull it away from my face. She drops the cloth and our fingers have closed around each other. There is silence. My heart pounds and I look at our hands. Zhen is looking too. Clocks have stopped – snow has halted its descent and hangs in mid-air, all the cars in this city have stopped, chopsticks are hovering frozen over food all over the city. There is only our hands.

But these moments always have to end. I don't know who really pulls away first, but our hands slip away, rest in our laps. There is silence, a silence that has spun itself around other directions, possibilities. It's too hot to touch, beyond words.

Time begins again, and with it I feel something new inside me.

I look into her eyes. 'You talk about wanting to help your father get out of this situation, but you don't talk about money. You are the only person who doesn't talk about it.'

Zhen looks deep into my eyes and summons the right words. Finally she says, 'I do want him out of here. My mother is sick because of it, my father looks like a fool, but…' She hesitates again, 'It can't be fixed with money with my father. His roots are here. I don't think you understand that because

74

foreigners like you don't have roots, you are blown about like seeds in the wind.'

I look at my hands and see mud in the nails, in the creases; this site has started to weld itself to my skin. Zhen doesn't know how painful it was to have my roots dug up and burnt. I feel a hollowness now, thinking about doing this to her father. 'I understand roots. That's all anyone wants.'

She looks away from me, out of the window, her eyes lost in the dying light. 'He would only leave if he could make the decision. Maybe he does it for my mother too. He saw what being a hero for the revolution can do to people.'

'But what do *you* want?' I spread my hands out in front of her. She looks at me, her gaze fixed. She searches my face and something there suggests that she has never been asked this before. This is the first time I allow myself to admit how beautiful she is to me – not just her outer shell but everything else.

It's then they arrive. Zhen's father bursts through the door rubbing his hands, a trail of snow swept up into the air behind him. A young man comes in with him and when he sees me, the man I quickly learn is Zhen's fiancé, stops still.

He seems to assess the scene carefully, take stock of where Zhen is in relation to me. Zhen mumbles something as she turns away to leave the room and he squints at my cheek and nods, looks a little more relaxed but he still hasn't moved. Almost as an afterthought, he thrusts out his hand to me. 'Nice to meet you. I'm Sun.'

As I smile politely I feel my face jab with pain and I instinctively move my hand to it. Behind Sun the last of the sunset has disappeared, and shadows are melting and expanding and becoming night.

'That looks nasty,' he mutters, but he neither moves further into the room nor sits down. Zhen comes back into the room with a cup of tea in an old enamel mug and Sun says something softly to her. She doesn't reply. She sits down on a chair away from me and cradles her tea in her hands. Her father looks from Sun to Zhen. There is a fragile silence that feels like it might shatter at any moment.

Sun moves forwards and takes the cup from Zhen's hand and speaks again. I sit up, sip at my tea and try not to notice. I want to leave but there is a tension in the room that I'm wound up in, like a fly in a web.

There is some hushed, frustrated exchange between them. Zhen's father stares at Sun now but when I glance at his face I can't read any emotion.

Zhen looks at me. 'Sun says he wants me to go with him to our place, but I have just explained to him that I am going to stay to look after my father and sick mother. Isn't that reasonable?'

I gulp tea and avoid any sort of answer. Sun looks from Zhen to her father and sighs. He grits his teeth.

'He's leaving now,' Zhen says to me, nodding in Sun's direction. I smile awkwardly, trying to avoid being caught up in the crossfire of this skirmish any more. It's then that a projectile crashes through the last front window, right next to me. Glass showers over my lap, splashes into my tea.

I peer out of the window and I see a dozen figures in black running towards the house. Some are throwing more objects in our direction. Zhen's father scurries back out of the front door with the speed of someone twenty years younger. Sun follows and Zhen and I scramble to get after them.

The whole site and surrounding block of streets is cloaked in an envelope of inky darkness now. Someone must have cut the power cables to the site. I have to stop where I am and let my eyes adjust. I run forwards off the bridge and fumble around for some sort of weapon and decide on a length of rough timber. I start swinging at anyone in black. I feel my legs wobbling and unsure with fear but adrenaline blasts into me and I keep swinging.

They are fast; they seem to know the site. I swing wildly a couple of times and eventually make contact with someone: I hear the sound of bone and flesh falling in front of me. I feel ecstatic. I have eliminated one person, but at the same time I feel a sense of horror that I may have hurt someone. It's a terrible mix of emotions.

I crouch, give myself time to catch my breath, wait for the pain in my chest to fade. The figure by my feet stirs and I am relieved he is alive. He sees me and attempts to crawl away. I have hurt his leg and he can't run. I look back. Zhen's house is behind me. The attackers are showering her house with projectiles, but do not target any other part of the site. I hear a whistle and as my eyes adjust completely to the dark I can see two or three figures limping away from Zhen's house back towards the site entrance, and the rest break off their attack and start running away. It seems the attack is over, that it was some sort of lightning strike.

The person at my feet tries to stand but can't and falls again. I listen for the sound of police sirens but I can't hear any yet. I look more closely at the thug. He seems like a small, thin man; not big for his role, but tough and sinewy. He is wearing a black balaclava. I get up, my knees still shaking and I take it off. His face is pinched; blood runs from the front of his head from a scratch. I tell him the police will be here soon but of course he doesn't understand me.

He starts to crawl away from me again then. I look around for lights but can still see no sign of police. If I wait for them to arrive he might manage to make his way to the street. I step forwards and grab him by the shoulder and pull him to his feet. He groans in pain but is too preoccupied to fight. I rest one of his arms around me and I take him back to Zhen's house to check his leg and wait for the police. I haven't had time to think about Zhen. I push down the panic that bubbles up when I think of her now, possibly hurt; I need to deal with this first.

I sit the man on the floor in the middle of the living room. I grab a kitchen knife and go towards his leg, intending to cut away his clothing to get a better look at the damage but he panics, backs away from me. I put the knife down slowly and point to the leg, trying to let him know I just want to check it. He seems to understand and he allows me to slowly roll up his trousers. He has a large gash down his calf. Blood drips onto the floor, fanning out onto the worn concrete. It looks like the wound only needs three or four stitches. I feel another wave of relief.

As I turn to pick up the knife and return to the kitchen he lunges towards the door. On the even surface he is remarkably fast and I have to slide across in front of him to prevent his escape. With no police here yet I start to think the unthinkable – how do I tie up a man?

I lock the front door and wave the knife at him so he moves back to the centre of the room. I put the weapon between my teeth so I have quick access and begin to scramble around the room looking for something I can restrain him with. Adrenaline is still pumping around my body and my hands shake as I rifle through piles of junk. I eventually have to settle for the cord of an old lamp. I tie his hands with it and lay the lamp beside him. I have to tie the cord three times – the first time I worry it's too tight and it might hurt him, the second time it's far too loose but the third time I seem to get a happy medium. His leg continues to bleed and a little more blood trickles onto the floor.

Panic for Zhen bubbles up once more. I get up and unlock the door, look back at my prisoner and step out into the darkness again to find her. As I take a few steps out of the house I see the three men I saw earlier walking towards me. No one is limping; no one seems to be in pain. I turn round, walk back into the house and collapse against the wall under the window. I am sitting on broken glass but I am too shocked to feel anything.

Some time later, my sense of time is hazy, jarred, Zhen's father enters the house, sees me and the figure on the floor and sighs. He then goes back out and yells into the darkness. Sun and Zhen come back in, breathless from running. Sun has a length of metal pipe in his hand that he throws outside behind him. Their eyes widen when they see the figure on the floor.

He is silent, staring at us all one by one. He struggles weakly against the lamp cord and I am relieved it holds. I can't see any clue to his feelings.

Zhen says to me, 'Are you all right?' I tell her I'm fine. I want to ask her the same but Sun looks at me and I have to content myself with a quick visual examination. She doesn't even seem to have a scratch. Sun is holding his shoulder but there is no blood. Zhen's father collapses into a chair and stares at the man again.

I say, 'Let's get the police. They should have been here already.'

Zhen and Sun sit near me on the floor. The colour has drained from both their faces. There is a sound outside and we all tense up, but it is just the wind.

'The police won't be that helpful. It might cause us trouble,' Sun says.

'What kind of trouble? We are the victims of an attack.'

Sun wipes some sweat off his face. 'Think about how it looks to them.'

I start to imagine the questions they will ask me, a foreigner who has taken a local prisoner. 'I know it doesn't look great, but surely when we explain...'

Zhen sighs. 'Sun's right. There are no witnesses, just one family's word against his.' She gestures at the man. We all look at him and he stares back at us. I'm not sure if I am imagining it, but I see the glimmer of a smile appear on his face, a look of satisfaction.

I run my hands through my hair. The enormity of what I have done hits me. I have a flashback to the contract I signed in the CEO's office, the agreement to not get involved in Chinese affairs. I look around the room at the shattered glass, the blood, the bound man and realise how bad this could be for all of us. I know now there may be a way out. 'The site does have some CCTV cameras. There will be images that could corroborate our story even if they don't show the attack on your house.'

Zhen pulls out her phone. 'That could just work.'

Sun tells her to stop as she starts dialling. 'What if the police have been paid off by the company? What if he *is* the police?' He motions at the prisoner.

I point outside. 'Then we take it to the press.'

'Good story...' Zhen starts, 'and there will be lots of trouble for them if that's true. But they will never forget our names.'

Sun says quietly to Zhen, but in English so I can understand, 'And what if it is the company, his company, that have hired them… He may even have known about it.'

I stop dead. Zhen's father looks at Sun and back at me. Zhen doesn't make eye contact with me.

'What?' I begin quietly. 'He attacked *me* as well.'

Zhen spits at Sun. 'What shit! He has tried to get a better deal for us. It doesn't make any sense.'

Sun shrugs, says, 'Either way, we can't take him to anyone.'

Zhen runs her hands through her hair. There is a long silence. We are all lost in our own thoughts. My thoughts seem to be going in ever-tightening circles, with no way out. Then Zhen says, 'Lindon, it's more than likely that it *is* your company who's hired these people, whoever they are. It's a tactic. This is the worst attack, but it has happened three times in the last few months.'

I lean forwards and let my head rest in my hands. I feel like the room is spinning slowly around me like a children's fairground ride. I want to get off but it doesn't stop. I have no words. Eventually, as the spinning slows down, I get up. I shake my head. 'We need to find out who did this tonight, but I refuse to believe it was the company.' I get up and walk towards their front door. I look back at the figure and say to Sun, 'Take a picture of him. Send it to me. I'm going to find out who these bastards are.' I move back to the man, stand next to him and hold his head facing Sun so he can get a clear shot. He holds his phone up at us and takes the images.

I move back towards the door, and push it open. 'It looks bad for everyone if I am here anyway. I'll go and walk a few blocks before I get a taxi.' I feel parts of my body ache now as the shock starts to wear off. All I want to do is sleep, to go far away.

Sun stands up and drags the prisoner up. 'I'll let our bastard go. I'll walk him out to the front and throw him into the gutter where he belongs.'

I walk for so long my feet hurt. I walk into the city, into garish neon and the currents of nightlife. It comforts me, wraps me up in something normal. I get a taxi home and when I take off my shoes they are full of blood. I sleep a long black sleep with no dreams. My dreams have been all taken from me, ripped away.

IV

Zhen

In the morning I help my father finish nailing wooden
panels over the window damaged in the last attack.
A small faded black-and-white wedding photo of my
parents by the window had fallen and shattered. I
rescue the old print. We lay it aside and we attach the
boards in place with rusty old nails he keeps in jars
on the kitchen windowsill. He says there is no point
in replacing the panes of glass as they will only get
smashed again next time. For once he talks common
sense. This is the last window in the living room and
as we finish the last board the room is cloaked in
darkness and even though it's mid-morning we have
to turn the light on. My father doesn't care about the
wedding photo. He leaves it on the floor.

I have scrubbed the floor where the attacker
lay, twice, but I still think I can see the traces of
mud where his body lay.

Sun tells me he let him go last night after I went to bed. He has been out on the roof making sure there are no more smashed roof tiles. He dusts the snow off as he enters and sits near me. I stare at the floor where the man was. Sun says, 'The foreigner is a double-headed snake. We can't deal with him any more.'

I look away from the spot on the floor. Some light manages to find its way through the narrow slivers of imperfection in the boards we have nailed up. 'He hasn't been here long enough to be like that. Who knows what he is,' I say. I have wanted to call him since last night, but haven't been alone.

Sun points at me. 'You can't trust foreigners.'

I sigh; I knew this was coming. 'You don't trust Shanghai people and you think Beijing people are arrogant. People are people. He is foreign: then he is foreign. It means nothing.'

'You are too trusting.' He mumbles something else half to himself about having work to do and he leaves the house abruptly. I would normally argue with him, but I am relieved when he is gone, surprised he didn't push his views onto me.

My mother comes home in the afternoon. She looks well rested and seems to walk more lightly. She looks at the newly boarded-up window and my father jumps in and says the wind blew the panes of glass out. She doesn't seem convinced by the lie. She smiles when she sees me, asks what I have eaten while she was in hospital. She scolds me when I say we have been eating out and heads straight for the kitchen, despite our protests.

Soon the smell of fried garlic and oil fills the house and it feels like home again. I go out to help my mother. She pushes a pile of bean sprouts at me, asks me to start pulling the tops off. I do this in silence for some time and then I feel her hand on my shoulder. She has stopped and says, 'When we were making the revolution, we had to fight for every li of ground, for every heart.'

I am startled by these words, uncomfortable. I want to just keep focused on the small delicate sprouts between my fingers but she stops me. She points at me now. 'You have more of my blood than your father's. You have a fighter's blood.'

I stammer, not sure where this is headed. I want her to stop. 'Mother, please...'

'We thought we could remake the world. I still think we can, but don't let the old world defeat you...' The finger she has pointed at me makes contact with my chest. 'I will be gone soon...'

I run from the kitchen, head for my room. I fumble for my phone and try to call Lindon, but each time I do my mother or father comes into the room and I hang up, my ears warm.

Sun comes back in the afternoon, looking distracted. He has taken the day off work and comes with flowers under his arm for my mother. I take them and tell him he shouldn't waste money on me and slap his arm but I am pleased more than I will say. He smiles as he greets my mother. Looks far away.

We eat lunch, talk about anything other than the house or the future. The battleground has grown quiet, cold. It is almost pleasant talking like this, like before.

Sun reminds me where we have to go today. After the events of last night I had forgotten and I suggest we cancel but he is right when he reminds me it took us two months to book it. I feel the afternoon darkening, decaying. The feeling uncoils itself inside me as I make my way out to Sun's car. Sun leaves first, but before I can follow my mother pulls my arm, stops me moving. I avoid her eyes, don't want to hear any more from her but she doesn't speak, she just shoves a book at me. I look down: it's an old scarred copy of Sun Tzu's *The Art of War*. When I look up at her to steal a glance there is something of a stubborn smile on her face.

The photographer yells at me, 'Hold still. Don't move.' I'm shivering too much. Wedding photos are so important they can't wait for the snow to thaw. In China we do them before the wedding, often months before. This photography studio is one of the best in the city; they started in Shanghai.

Sun says without moving his lips, 'Quick photo, then warm coat.'

There's a light dusting of snow on the ground in

front of us. We look like plastic wedding figurines on an iced white cake in an American movie. We have tacky Western costumes on. This is something we argued about when we booked all this. I wanted a Tang dynasty dress. Sun said that was not cultured. We are posing in front of a small purpose-built Western-style chapel. Hundreds of people have their photos taken here each weekend. This is theatre, all theatre now. It reminds me of one of those old propaganda films.

An image of Lindon pushes itself into my mind as I pose – it produces a twisted yarn of feeling that excites and repels me. Why do I think of him now? I try and blink his image away. I rearrange my skirt to keep my eyes busy, but it doesn't work. The photographer's assistant runs around behind me and pulls the coat from around my shoulders. Another young guy does the same for Sun and catches the flower in his lapel, which flies off across the snow. The boys scamper back out of view. I am standing in the snow in a white wedding gown, lace falling into the ice. Sun has a white tuxedo with purple bow tie. We both plaster silly grins across our faces. We hide other feelings.

I take a deep breath to still my body and say, 'A warm coat sounds like heaven.' More camera clicking, and we are moved into new positions. Sun kneels in front of me and I have to lean against him with my hands clasped around his shoulders like a brooch. He strokes my hand when it's in position and I try to feel something, but the feelings are blurred, hard to attach words to describe them.

More and more people are watching us, shaming me. I feel tired and cold now, with a cold that's got inside under my skin. I mutter to Sun, 'I told you people would stare.'

Through the big artificial grin stuck on his face he mutters back, 'It's cheaper.'

'They all think I'm pregnant. Why else would we have photos done in the fucking snow?'

Sun swings around to face me. He wants to say something, I can see words that bubble up close to the surface, but he can't get them out. I have caught him off guard. The photography crew, and now some bystanders, are watching. Sun catches them out of the corner of his eye and slowly his face stiffens and the emotion ebbs away. He turns back to face the camera but he looks disturbed, drained of colour.

A boy comes out to readjust Sun's hair, plaster it back up into some kind of shape. Sun mutters, 'You said it's romantic with the snow...' but his voice trails off. He can't finish his sentence.

The boy runs back. I say to Sun, 'Romantic?' I regret being so sharp with my words. I know how much they will hurt him. One of my high heels slips and the side of my shoe closest to Sun falls a couple of centimetres, shaky foundations. I can't even manage to stand in these damned heels.

The photographer yells at us, 'Look at the camera, talk later!' and our heads snap back into position.

We move to the door of the chapel, kneel beside each other for another shot.

The cameramen are a few metres back. They want to capture the building for the shot. I let loose the words that have been ready to fire all morning, 'Let's not buy the flat.' I look over at Sun; his eyes wince slightly, he puts his hand up to the photographers to stop them, tells them we need a five-minute break. Coats are draped over us. The crew huddle away from us, light cigarettes.

'You know we need a place of our own. We don't want to waste our money paying rent to someone else—'

I cut him off, rest a hand on his arm. 'I know all that. What I mean is, let's just leave it for a while.' I add softly while I look down at his sleeve, 'We can travel, go west.'

Sun laughs. 'But we have work, I have a career here.'

'We can still do our jobs, but I've been thinking I'd like to do something.'

'What?' He frowns at me.

'See places.' I add quickly, 'It will be harder later with kids.'

Sun smiles. 'That's romantic, but I don't know about the timing…'

'Haven't you ever wanted to wander, walk the earth?'

He laughs, pats my head like a child. 'It would be nice but we are not students, we have obligations – schools for our kids, old parents. Our parents aren't rich.'

My fingers ache with cold and I can't hold the flowers any more. I drop my small bouquet, delicate purple petals on long green stems. They fall onto the ice, lost in white. I look at them as the camera flashes at us and we begin again.

When it's all over we go home. Sun says he wants to stay with me at my parents' tonight. People in the street see us walking close, exchanging small talk. I see how difficult things are for him. He carries heavy burdens. My obligations to my family have me in a vice as well. If I walk away from him it will bring great shame on everyone. My fate has swerved out of my control. Can anyone really control their destiny?

I find myself in bed with Sun, wanting to walk, to run. I think about Lindon again, imagine if he were here. But I remind myself that foreigners like to play, they aren't solid. They divorce, fuck around. I rest my head against Sun's shoulder and he puts his head on mine. When he thinks I am asleep he rolls over and sobs quietly. I have never heard him cry before. I think about the wedding photo on the floor; it's the last thing I see as I am swallowed in sleep.

*

Lindon

I sit outside the CEO's office in a mud-stained suit staring at the model. Many of those small pigeonholes will be filled with newlyweds whose families have kindly sunk their savings into their new homes. The more I stare at the model the more imperfections I see in it; I even wonder if the model has deteriorated since I last looked at it. I think of the first place Julie and I bought, purchased with hard-earned overtime money. The hardest part about divorce, after the scar tissue starts to form, is the houses sold and split, funds siphoned by one partner, retirement funds lost. Julie emptied our accounts and liquidated our assets very cleverly before I even knew she was leaving; the walls and objects that held together my life were auctioned off, stripped off me.

She is the reason I am here, in the middle of this shit storm. I hate her even more now.

The CEO's PA sits in the waiting room opposite me, preening herself. We are bathed in music and beige walls. There is no sense of urgency about what she does – there is a timelessness in the way she straightens her hair and checks her nails. She has probably never had mud on her shoes.

Her desk is pristine and soulless – no personal photos, no mementos. The only thing that makes her desk any different from any other are the two small flags – one Chinese and one American, to symbolise the relationship between the American CEO and his Chinese staff – that she has set in a small wooden stand.

I have made this appointment three times over the last two days, and each time I have cancelled because it takes me two days to work out exactly what I should say, to curate my language.

I scan the table in front of me for a magazine to flick through, find a distraction of some kind and I see a small creased paperback book on the edge of the table. I pick it up and the cover's title makes me smile: *The Art of War* by Sun Tzu. I open the front cover, start to scan the first page, but the PA's phone interrupts my reading and I look up at her. All she says into the receiver is, 'OK,' and she nods at me. I tuck the paperback into my jacket pocket and head towards the CEO's office.

It's like the boardroom – there is a large plastic-looking plant, a couple of academic certificates in frames and not much else; the whole thing looks makeshift, like a film set that could be packed up and trucked to a new location in half an hour. The CEO stands as I enter and gestures to the chair. He gives me a sympathetic look as I sit before him. He accentuates this by leaning forwards. He says, tone hushed, 'I heard what you got caught up in the other night. Really sorry, we are all very glad that you are unharmed.'

I nod. 'Thank you, but really it was over very quickly.'

He clasps his hands in front of him and bites his bottom lip, then says, 'What we need to do now is make sure that you are safe, that you can move ahead with your very crucial role here with us.'

'I appreciate that very much—' I begin.

He sits back in his chair, smiles, changes his tone and cuts me off with, 'In fact, we have located your own office next to the boardroom and have organised some escorts trained with safety in mind to make sure you are OK. First and foremost, it is my job to see that everyone in our team, everyone from the cleaner to people like yourself, are able to do what you do best. And do that in safety.' He smiles at the end of this, satisfied. There is a dissonant finality in his words, a sound that says 'this is the end', a 'full stop'. Is he waiting for me to leave?

'Actually, about the other night…'

The smile drops and he looks concerned again. 'You can be forgiven for being caught in this kind of situation. You are new to doing business here. Put it behind you—'

I cut him off now, leaning forwards. 'Well, to put this behind me I would hope that we, as a company, ensure that this kind of attack on one of our sites is investigated.'

He looks irritated, checks his watch. 'I have a team of investigators out there now, interviewing local residents. We are handling this in the most appropriate way and let me assure you that we will resolve this issue.'

I have the feeling that I am caught in the middle of a very well-prepared routine. I brush my trousers and mud from the site dust drifts off into the air and catches the light – it almost looks beautiful, peaceful as it floats there. 'So you have contacted the police?'

He bristles at the word police but tries to hide his reaction behind a masked smile. 'Now, you have to understand the way things are done here, the business culture. Involving the police in what is a very complex issue might inflame the situation. I'm sure you don't want to see the situation fester further?'

I remember the glass in my tea, running blindly, swinging a piece of wood. It seems unreal. 'People could have been hurt.'

He puts his hand up. 'Luckily no one *was* harmed, and it was over quickly. I have to remind you that we are in a tenuous position here. There are laws around these issues that we as foreigners need to be careful of. There's one charge often used that is called something like "picking quarrels and provoking troubles". Getting involved in these things could put the whole project in doubt.'

I look at my shoes. I wonder if the mud will ever come out of my clothes, my life. I change tack. 'I hope your investigations have borne fruit. I want to know who did this.'

He bites his lip again, lowers his voice. 'These kinds of incidents can be a regular part of the real estate game here, I'm afraid. Just keep focused on your work. Press conferences, PR – we need your face and of course your skills. In fact I have organised...'

He talks about a press conference he has arranged to announce a new release of apartments across town, a new project. He pours out the details excitedly and I nod and smile and do all the things considered 'professional and engaged', but underneath I grow cold.

I leave the office in a daze, lost in my own thoughts. His PA catches me at the lift. She introduces me to two men in dark suits. I go through the motions and smile and grasp their hands firmly. I'm so wrapped up in my own thoughts I don't hear everything she says and when she finishes I say goodbye to the men. One frowns and the other smiles.

The lift doors open, I step in and they follow me. I say in English, not expecting a reply, 'You are off too?'

The one on the left takes a pair of designer sunglasses out of his pocket and slowly puts them on. He says, 'Of course, we go where you go.'

I then recall the conversation with the CEO – the 'escorts'. I wonder why, if these men are here simply to protect me, they would need to speak English. I look out at the city as we descend; it is serene on the outside. I notice the snow is melting. Inside I begin to burn – Zhen was right about who I work for. I have been fooled before but I won't let that happen again. I run numbers through my head, keep trying to justify why I am here and how many numbers I will gain.

But the burning grows bigger, and the numbers are dirty.

I buy two large bottles of beer, retreat to my hotel room and gaze out of the window for a while, drinking slowly from one of the bottles in the hope that the liquid will extinguish the anger inside. I feel a weight in my jacket and pull out *The Art of War* I'd picked up earlier. I flip through the pages, idly at first, then spend the rest of the afternoon absorbed in its musty yellowing pages. Maybe I am in the middle of a war, a battle ground? If so '…this is hemmed-in ground.'

*

Zhen

I will say goodbye to Lindon today. I must. Sun is a steady man. He is a good match and I can't throw all that away.

The banner is unfurled as Lindon, 'the foreigner', and I walk across the land bridge towards the gate.

Lindon is in mid-sentence and we both stop, our attention seized by the blaze of red that falls from the crane. At the top of the machine three workers clamber around and secure the fabric to the bottom of the operator's platform as it thrashes around in the wind. They look precarious, fragile. The banner falls towards the ground and harmlessly strikes a large LPG gas tank by the base of the crane.

Lindon asks, even more agitated now, 'What do the characters say?' He has been anxious all morning. He has been glancing back at the escorts behind him. They walk like robots. They seem to be listening, so Lindon mumbles and I strain to hear. They look up at the banner as well, seemingly interested.

'They say they are protesting about last month's unpaid wages.'

Lindon runs his hands through his hair. 'That's all we need,' he says under his breath.

I want to talk to Lindon, to walk and talk with him for the whole of the morning. But the heaviness of what I have to say to him weighs on me. Each step is sticky and heavy. We walk on towards the site entrance.

Lindon asks, 'The man we had… you know…?' He looks at the escorts again as he says this. They are fixed on the banner, not listening.

I look out towards the road; I want to avoid the hurt I will feel looking into his eyes. Avoid other feelings I dare not name. 'Sun let him go,' I say, knowing what he refers to.

He looks disappointed, deflated. 'He didn't say anything, did he?'

'I don't know. Not while I was with them.' I take a deep breath and fold my arms. It feels colder today. The ice seems to be burying its needles into my skin. It's always like that when the snow melts. I bite my lower lip now; I know I just need to say it. 'Lindon, I have to tell you…' I stop again, collect my thoughts.

He looks into my eyes. I can see tiredness hanging under them.

'Soon I will have to do something very important, as you know, I guess—'

He cuts me off. 'I'm worried about you. I want you to move your family into a hotel. You don't need to worry about expenses. The company will take care of all that.'

I pause, readjust. I didn't expect this. It distracts me.

'If we do that,' I respond, 'they will finish destroying the house.'

Lindon looks out over the pit, not at me. He is far away. 'This is my project, this is my site, I won't let that happen.'

I make the mistake of touching his arm. I know this will make things more difficult, but my body does it without me agreeing. I say, 'Lindon, I believe you wouldn't. But with us not here they would find a way. One push of a machine and the walls of the house would tumble over.'

He grinds his teeth, and I pull him by the arm and we continue towards the entrance. I am growing nervous that Sun will come home and see me like this with Lindon. I want to say this terrible thing and move on.

I say it quietly. 'My wedding is in a couple of days, I need to focus on that.'

I sense him harden, stiffen. I didn't expect such an obvious reaction. It hurts me more. He says quietly, 'Of course. But after that we can meet together and work on a way forward.'

We get to the entrance. The street is a few metres away. A glance behind and the escorts have stopped, mercifully a little way behind us. I wonder how much of this they are following, or can read from our body language. I turn away from Lindon and look back at my father's house and say, 'I don't think I can be involved with you, in this, any more. It's complicated.'

There is a silence. A silence in which I am

aware of the sound of machine rigging moving, traffic in the distance, chatter on the street. The world grinds on around us but we are sharing our last moment together in it. The silence seems to last a small lifetime.

'I wish you all the best,' he says, so quietly it's almost like a whisper on the wind. I hear him stride away towards the road. The escorts walk past me, impassive but somehow menacing in the way they walk. I worry about him now. What new threats will now follow him around? I feel hollowed out, empty.

But this is my fate.

Children play with fireworks, set off crackers around the machines. They sound like guns, weapons. I flinch. I watch the workers on the top of the crane, wonder what it feels like to topple from a great height and have the ground rush up to end the pain and uncertainty.

*

Lindon

We are in a KTV room now, walls studded with plastic imitation diamonds. Frank is here – he has ordered girls and our clients look happy with cigarettes stuck out of their mouths and wine flowing like a river into their glasses. He wears glasses without lenses, making him clown-like, a circus character. There's no conversation, only a fog of pleasure, drink and murdered melody.

I drink quickly, down three half-glasses of Chinese

white wine. I think about Zhen Yi, imagine her wedding. My feelings for her have crept up on me, grown in some secret corner and it frightens me. I drink again. It makes me gasp but the third drink is soft, makes my head light; thoughts become watercolour paint. I want to get lost in wine, forget.

A girl with short spiky hair and tall dangerous-looking heels is lounging on the lap of an investor from Germany; he is reclined on a sofa his hands all over her, exploring her, restlessly looking for something. There's a guy beside him who sits cradling a drink, his eyes lost in the images on the TV. He looks somewhere else, removed from us. My escorts remain outside, giving me at least this sordid corner of privacy.

The room smells sour and musty and old. Frank has his hand up the skirt of a girl with long dark hair with a large beauty spot near her top lip who resists and tries to pull his hand away, but it's so half-hearted it's almost funny. He keeps kissing the beauty spot and the girl blushes each time, or seems to blush, and I wonder if the spot is real because it seems so perfect and round and dark. I stare at her lip and ignore the girl beside me, who smells like too much cheap perfume but is perfectly shaped in all the right places. I don't know who the rest of the people are and I don't know what we should be discussing. I drink more wine and watch hands on legs, admiring how pleasure-seeking early Chinese capitalism is, how seductive.

A girl leans over, a KTV girl, and subtly pulls

down her top so that her cleavage catches my eye and she says, breaking my eyes away from the other girl's beauty spot, 'You are so handsome you must have many, many women.'

I push her away. 'That would be too complicated.'

She zeros in on me again. She runs her hand up my thigh and my body reacts to the warmth of her breasts against me and her skin is soft against my neck. She doesn't need to be told she's beautiful; it's her trade. Thoughts of concrete evaporate; I welcome the distraction from the deep dark hole that's devouring me but I stop her. I move away to get another glass of wine. She pulls out a compact mirror and checks her make-up.

Frank pushes 'his girl' down towards his crotch by the hair. They all laugh but he pushes too hard and I say to her, straining my voice above the music, 'Maybe you can get us some food. How about some meat-on-sticks?' and the men clap their hands. My head is spinning. I manage to pull 'Frank's girl' away from him and push her out of the door but he grabs her shirt.

Frank looks at me like a child whose toy has been taken away. 'She was my fun.'

I stumble. Lean on the lounger next to me for support. There's something about his sneer that gets me. I'm not a fighter, not in this way – I've never hit a man, never wanted a fight, but now I do. My fingers twitch, I flex them. 'Let her go.'

Frank laughs, looks around the room. No one is

paying much attention to us yet, he has maintained his 'face'. He says, 'I'll find another then...' and he lets her go. He says he's going to pee. I get up, lurch towards the door after him, see him as he is about to disappear into the bathroom.

'Hostile armies may face each other.' I don't intend to yell down the corridor, but it tumbles out anyway. 'I know what you have done.'

He stops, turns his flushed face to me. He appraises me for a moment. 'You are very funny, Mr Lindon. A very funny man.'

I move closer to him. He takes a step towards me, cautious. I lower my voice. 'You just pay people off, buy your way through every obstacle.'

He studies my face, waits before replying. We can hear muffled laughter squeezed out around closed doors mixed with distant voices. He says very quietly, 'You must have read a story somewhere. I wouldn't do that.'

I snigger. 'I have seen you myself, first-hand...' I tell him about the banquet, seeing him with the envelope full of cash that was exchanged. I add enough other descriptive detail that his face twitches nervously; he knows I'm not making it up.

'What about you?' he asks and shoves his hands into his pockets. He is smiling again, calm.

I'm sobering up; sobering up in a variety of ways. 'What about me? I haven't paid off safety inspectors.'

'How different are you from me?' He steps close, lowers his voice still further; he looks like he is taunting me, probing my defences.

'I couldn't be more different.'

'Really? You are paid big dollars by the company to come to my country to do what? To make as much cash out of us as you can and then take off. Use your white face to look good. If you really cared you would leave now. Take whatever inflated salary you have been paid and run.' I feel a knot in my stomach, I stutter on a reply but find it hard to pull my thoughts together.

I'm prickly with doubt. I try to answer. 'I am more than qualified to lead a project... It's not that simple.'

He shrugs. 'I lived in the UK for three years when my English wasn't so good. I know what it's like to be a fish out of water. So you couldn't get your translator to call the police and dob me in? What held you back if you are such a good man?'

'How can you pay bribes that put people at risk?'

He laughs. 'If I hadn't, someone else would have done. This is the way things are – this is business.'

'You disgust me,' I say. But I am also disgusted with myself.

He stops smiling, comes forwards, right to my face. I'm too drunk to be nervous. I can smell the sweat on his skin. I feel him breathing hard right in front of me. We both smell stale like rotten, sour beer. He says very quietly – I almost have to strain to hear – 'Don't talk such shit to me. Do you know what my mother did? They used to farm rice, while quotes of Chairman Mao were broadcast over speakers.

The only book my father read when I was growing up was the little red one. The Party privatised the hospitals and we couldn't even get medical care any more. Foreigners came in and feasted on the carcass of our dying ideas. They can only make such good money off the back of our poverty. That's what my mother got for being married to a dreamer.'

I can't look at him now. I look at the carpet, trace patterns in it. I actually start to feel a small pang of pity for him. This scrambles my response. I lean against the wall, all of a sudden tired, disorientated again. I am part of this?

He says, 'I have to make *my* way. I can't feed my child with nice ideas, buy him a house with Mao's thoughts or pay our medical expenses with ideology. What happens if I don't do what I have to do? Someone else will, and I will be swept aside. I have to swim in the sea or drown. You are getting your building done quickly, so don't try and teach me about being good. You will be gone soon anyway, you are a shadow on the wall here.' He walks away, slowly, doesn't look back. I suddenly feel like throwing up; it's not just the alcohol, it's something else, a choking feeling.

I stand in the corridor staring ahead for a while, I don't know how long. I try to call Zhen Yi but her phone goes to voicemail.

Frank's words echo inside me. I want to run, clear my head. I notice then that my escorts aren't here; they must have been lured to another room to drink.

I look for an exit I won't be spotted using and see the fire exit sign at the end of the corridor. I move unsteadily towards it and hear a door open behind me. I spin round and hear something fall from my jacket but I can't see what it is in the gloom. I look towards the door then and see it's the girl who had been all over me earlier. She smiles and moves towards me. I ignore her and flee down the fire escape.

The door swings shut and it's a relief not to hear the music. I use the handrail for support and shuffle down the concrete stairs. I hear the fire exit door, now a floor or two above me, close and the sound of heels echo around me. I hear the girl call to me but I ignore her. I rush out into the icy night air and find a taxi, to escape. Is Frank right, should I just go? Am I the mud that dirties this place, dirties Zhen's life? But as I fall into a car and I'm asked where I want to go to, doubt swamps me. I recall Frank's words, '*You will be gone soon anyway, you are a shadow on the wall here.*' The driver asks me again where I want to go. He seems impatient. I have two destinations in mind. I am at a fork in the road.

The woman has caught up and she bangs on the window beside me, waves at me. I blurt out one of those destinations, a decision made – numbers won't control me, not any more.

V

*'Amid the turmoil and tumult of battle, there may be
seeming disorder and yet no real disorder at all...'*
                    The Art of War, Sun Tzu, Chapter 5, 16

Zhen

I jump when the first fireworks at the hotel entrance explode next to us. We are standing too close. I hear my phone rumble in my bag but I don't check it, I can't. Sun has insisted, without actually insisting, that I wear heels and they have already cut into the backs of my feet. They are bleeding and my stockings are glued to my skin with blood.

Three-metre-high posters of us in Tang dynasty dress hang from the entrance as we walk in, escaping the crackers. Sun and I stand just inside the hotel lobby door greeting guests. As we bow we are like waxwork figures that bend at the waist. My heart feels hard and plastic, I feel nothing.

'Smile, darling, smile,' Sun mutters through closed teeth. We wear exhausted smiles but try to look happy. I have heavy layers of make-up on to make me into something presentable for a wedding.

Already the room is misty with smoke. A girl in a red traditional *qi pao* guides us past tables of old people to our table at the side, near the exit sign. Young people are all sitting here, some we know, some we have half met sometime but not well enough to know what to say. They look marooned, adrift on a life raft. Sun starts smoking and asking the couple next to us about the food. They say it's good. All the dishes are local with lots of meat. Sun looks happy.

Dishes arrive, plates of peanuts, pickled vegetables and plates of cold black fungi that look like black leaves soaking in a dark sauce.

We negotiate our way from the back of the room to the front. People continue to talk, but they watch us. I have changed into a new dress, as is the custom; I wear the Tang dress featured on the poster outside. It's tight, badly fitted and cuts into my skin. I watch all this like I am watching a film, like this is someone else's wedding.

Up on a small stage, we are directed into place. It is lit with small coloured spotlights, and decorated with huge styrofoam 'double happiness' characters that have been hung slightly crooked. A small flowering of fireworks explodes from the stage as we move into the correct position, and the 'host' jumps out, wearing a sequinned jacket. He starts to introduce us like we are strangers to our family. It's all too loud, but they always do this. It's the only way people can hear over the conversations that still go on. Noise is lucky.

The small explosions and the smell of the gunpowder

draw me back into myself. Bring me back to earth. This is really happening; it is my event. These 'double happiness' paper cut-outs are supposed to be for me. Eyes are on me... It's all real.

I look out beyond the lights and see Mei smoking. All my other friends are smiling but she can see how I'm really feeling and she doesn't smile. She knows I am an unhappy bride. I realise suddenly I'm caught in other people's dreams.

It's hot in here. I loosen my top button, and feel the relief of cool air hitting my skin. Sun's cheeks are red from beer. I haven't touched any. I feel sick already. The smoke around me makes me want to light a cigarette of my own, but Sun hates me smoking, I can't let him see me do that.

The host is making my head hurt. He is telling jokes and has us playing games with apples and white wine and the usual tricks. As I twist with Sun, close to him, I think about Lindon. The old relatives at the back find the jokes funny, they laugh and chuckle. I wince, wish for this to be over.

Two entire families; friends at the edge, and the oldest and dearest of the bloodline at the back and middle. I look out between camera flashes and cheers and see everyone we love in front of us. Tables of friends, close family, cousins we never see much. I get glimpses of them eating and smoking and toasting and I realise they are here mainly for themselves. It's really only our parents who seem interested in us, and I see them straining against the noise and the light to watch us. There is a big bank of lights on us like we are on a film set and we start to sweat, my make-up runs.

A rapper jumps out from the wings of the stage and starts rapping about love. It's a traditional Chinese poem that's been butchered into modern rhyme. Sun laughs, sees the humour in it. The rapper leaps down in amongst the tables and white and silver showers of sparks explode from the back of the stage. I turn to him, hot and tired and say, my face fixed in a show-smile for the audience, 'I told you I didn't want a rapper.'

'It's fun, we have to keep everyone entertained.'

'This is *our* wedding. My ideas don't count for much.'

'They do, of course they do. But we have to think of others,' Sun says.

'Who thinks of me?'

'What?'

'You love me, I know that, but you don't love the important parts of me.' My parents hear this, start to stir, push some other family members away from us so no one can hear.

Sun laughs. 'I love all of you.'

I raise my voice, 'If you had loved us…'

Sun goes red, but doesn't shrink from the challenge. 'Then what? Say what you have to say.' The DJ turns up the music, tries to distract people with some jokes. He anxiously signals for a spotlight to follow him.

Sun pushes me away towards the side of the room. My father just stares at us. He can't move. Sun yells in my face, 'It's the foreigner, isn't it?'

Flashes from cameras go off as the DJ grabs some close family to come up and play games. In between flashes of photos I see the exit sign clear against black background at the end of the room.

Sun tightens his grip on my arm. 'We have known each other for so long. Our whole families are here. We love each other.'

I smile and snort. 'How can love grow amongst secrets, lies?'

He frowns, lets go of my arm, 'I have no secrets from—'

I point at him. 'If you loved me you wouldn't continue, even now, to lie to me.'

The DJ makes a joke and everyone laughs. Sun turns slightly, worried they are laughing at him. Tightness grips my heart. I feel a growing sense that a thousand *jin* of water is bubbling up over me and I think I see Lindon in the crowd, smiling, but it's a guest I don't know.

Sun pushes me further from our guests, desperate for this fight to take place on safer ground but I stand firm. He says, 'I have worked day and night to provide for you. For your family and mine.'

I hear fireworks as an explosion comes from the stage. Red confetti showers over us and falls all through my hair. I can't breathe. I clutch my phone, stare at the screen and I see the exit sign behind me glowing again. 'Our job is to be honest with each other. What about your hidden messages, why can't you tell me where you go?'

Sun seems to forget where he is, flushes red in the face. 'Where *I* go? You are the one who seems to be spending all your time with another man! What are *you* not telling me?'

Words evaporate momentarily, feelings bubble in me, risk taking over. I think of Lindon, think of the lies I am telling myself. The biggest lies aren't those we tell to others, but those we can't see in ourselves. I step back, make fists with my hands and bury them in my dress so he can't see. I layer my anger over thoughts of Lindon. '*You* disappear for "work", delete messages on your phone. It was never like this. We had time before.'

Sun reaches out for me and I flinch. 'I am involved in a special project... I need to make money while I can.'

I take a step back again, retreat. 'We can't make a marriage with walls of money.'

'We can't live without it. This world only knows money now. Are you blind?'

I see the time I have been with Sun flash before me. The embraces, the meals, the tears. He has changed, and a sadness overwhelms me at the death of that time, of *that* Sun. I move towards the exit sign, have to pass Sun as I do. It feels like my soul is being torn into shreds, each going a different way but I trust my feet now. I say to Sun as I pass him, 'It's not someone else. It's easier to blame someone else. I just want something different, of my own.'

My father has slipped up beside us. I didn't notice him move in the confetti and the noise. He puts his hand on Sun's hand and Sun releases me, surprised.

My father looks into Sun's eyes, then at me. He nods at me with the hint of a smile and I feel an avalanche of tears begin to form but I hold them back.

I hitch my skirt up, dash for the exit door. It creaks and yawns and I am gone, down the stairs. I find myself lost, run into an exit that's locked and collapse on the floor. A bird in a corner, flapping its wings, looking for an open window, a gust of wind.

I hear footsteps behind me. I squeeze my eyes shut, hoping to block this out, the looming confrontation. The steps come closer, stop. They are heavy, weighed down with sadness. I wonder what Sun will say when I turn round, if he will hit me. I bow my head, put my hands on the door hoping it will open. I give it a small nudge, and of course it just stays there. Mocks me. Then I feel it, a gentle touch on my shoulder and I turn, force my eyes open. It's my father again. I thought it would be my mother and I stare at him. He pushes at the door, uses his weight to force it open. He points at the open exit and just says, 'Go, little Zhen.'

The cold air floods through my clothes but I don't care. I am running, I am free, out of the little cage door. Out onto the street and I disappear into the night, running into the snow. My father has helped uncage me, maybe he does care about something more than that old pile of bricks? Has my mother sent him on her errand?

The taxi driver I eventually hail when I can run no more looks startled when he sees this hysterical-looking woman in a wedding dress. I smile, thinking of Lindon.

I will go to him now, follow my own path.

I turn on my phone and try to call Lindon before I arrive back at the site. I see he has tried to call me but his phone is ringing out now. I imagine him in bed, asleep. I leap out of the taxi when I arrive, throw off my heels so I can navigate my way through the melting muddied snow. The freezing liquid hurts my toes, but the pain is distant. I am halfway to his apartment building when a woman starts shouting behind me. I stop and take the time to catch my breath. I notice the cold on my skin through the flimsy dress. It presses in on me.

'Do you know the foreigner?' she yells, stumbling in my direction and waving a phone at me. She looks like a whore, painted in bright colours and wearing slutty clothes.

'Why do you ask?' I call Lindon again, look away from her up into Lindon's flat. The windows are black pools – still, dead.

The phone lights up in her hand, 'I want to give him this, he left it in the room.'

I recognise the phone, squint as I make my way towards her and see my name on the screen. I feel like retching into the mud beside me, feel sickness from deep within me. So he is one of *those* foreigners, he has been with whores. I snatch the phone. My breath is gone, has been robbed from me.

She says, 'Hey, this isn't yours, I want to give it to the foreigner.'

'It's not yours either. I know him, and I will give him the phone,' I yell at her.

She looks me up and down, folds her arms. 'Your business then.'

I turn, my head spinning with anger, nowhere to go. She says, laughing, 'He was obviously so happy to marry you he was singing songs and drinking with me. He muttered something about the airport when I last saw him. What a great husband!'

I spin round and slip towards the road, my toes numb and in pain. I catch up with the slut in a few strides and push her sideways into the mud. She screams as I lurch towards a curious taxi driver who has slowed down to watch our drama. I tell him to drive fast, that I will give him double the meter if he can get to the airport faster. He stares at me with wide eyes, quite likely thinking me mad. It's not until I pull out some cash from my bra and throw it at him that he turns and the car moves away from the kerb.

I am consumed with an anger I didn't know I could feel. He won't do this to my heart. I will make him pay before he can escape.

*

Lindon

I watch the second aircraft I have seen tonight touch down outside. Airports are wonderful places – they feel like they belong to no country. They are like seams adjoining sections of fabric. The planes, huge impossible-looking structures, glide gracefully to earth in a steady rhythm I find comforting.

People in airports are either dressed in corporate 'uniforms' of some kind, or their best comfortable clothes. I am dressed in a suit streaked with rain and ice and salt and have left an icy brown signature on the fabric bench I am sitting on. I look like a wreck but because I am a foreigner I only get watchful glances, wide berths. If I was a local they would think I'm mad or homeless.

It is here I have come to face my future, to do the calculations about what lies ahead. I occupy a no man's land in this nondescript lounge in the centre of the airport between the international ticket booking office and the exit from the building – two futures separated by a couple of hundred metres.

I have bought three large plastic bottles of water and ten packets of Japanese sweet Pokey sticks in an effort to sober up completely as I chew over possibilities. I am half way through the second bottle of water and chase the liquid down with a couple of painkillers in anticipation of another hangover. I think of Zhen, who appears in some impossible future and I scramble vainly for my phone to hear her voice but I curse when I realise I have lost the phone somewhere. Probably stolen by the sugary fingers of the whore I was with. Another future obliterated, another departure lounge closed.

The painkillers and water have started to clear my head and I get up to walk, to order my thoughts. I should go back to the ticket counter and buy a ticket to somewhere, anywhere but here; but Zhen

Yi is in this city, and I can't let go of the images of her that have planted roots inside me. I move to the window away from my chair and watch another plane glide down towards the runway in front of me and gently come to rest on the landing strip. I imagine her with me on that plane touching down somewhere far away from here. Another impossible daydream I can't shake. I turn and watch the aircraft slowing down as it moves away from this building.

Out of the corner of my eye I see someone very close to me and as I twist my head I recognise Sun. He motions to my chair – I think he can tell it was where I was sitting by the trail of muddy shoe prints that lead back there. I walk slowly with him back to the mess and he sits down quietly beside me after brushing his chair down with his hand. He is dressed in a grey suit, white shirt and blue bow tie; his shoes are shiny, impeccable, hair pressed back. He stares straight ahead, very assured. Still. I want to ask him about the wedding but sense this would be a mistake.

The first thing he says is, 'You are at an airport with no bags.'

I swig some more water. Sun is rubbing his clean hands like there is mud he can't see.

'Do I look like I'm dressed for flying?' I say.

He smiles, a pained half-smile. 'You look like shit.'

I nod in agreement. Another plane comes in and begins to land. The lights flash by us as it begins to slow. 'I find airports a good middle ground. Nice place to think.'

Sun turns to me. 'I'm glad you weren't planning on leaving. That would have disappointed a few people tonight.' He reaches into his pocket and brings out his phone but doesn't check it. He leaves it in his lap.

I mumble, more to myself than him, 'I don't think my departure would disappoint anyone.' The plane has stopped and small service vehicles ease out towards the aircraft. I wonder where the plane has come from.

I look at him, say, 'In fact I think it would have made a lot of people's lives a little simpler.'

Sun nods and says, very quietly, 'I have something to show you.' His phone is activated; there is an image there, but I don't look down at first. I take another swig of my water and challenge him. 'It seems a bit strange that you would find me here, at the airport. How would you know I am here at all?'

Sun leans forwards. 'A couple of months ago I was headhunted away from my old company. I was in charge of public relations for a chemical company that dealt with multinational interests. Then I got an offer I couldn't refuse. It gave me the deposit for Zhen's and my flat in a few short months.' I study his eyes, look for a betrayal of emotion but there appears to be none. 'We share the same employer.'

I breathe in a big lungful of air and exhale. 'Explains...' I begin to say. Things start to click together. '...how the CEO, the day I saw him, knew so much.'

Sun smiles, smug, in control. I pick up a bottle of my water and swig a huge mouthful. I feel coldly, suddenly, sober. I lean forwards now. Our heads are close together; I can smell some expensive chemical-induced sweet odour. 'So are you hired to watch me, or harass Zhen's family?'

Sun's smile fades slightly. 'We would never be associated with violence. I didn't physically watch you, but I was brought in to help monitor the situation with you. My connection to Zhen's family certainly helped. I checked contracts and talked to locals. It seemed like easy money and mutually beneficial for me and the company, but...' his voice drops, 'then you got to know my *fiancée*. A little too well...'

I watch passengers slowly assembling in our area ready for boarding their flight. Children look excited and business people check computers and phones. I turn to Sun. 'Zhen said that after her wedding day she would never see me again. As someone told me tonight,' I add, with wry irony, 'I'm only a shadow on the wall now. So why are you actually here?'

Sun leans close to my ear, lowers his voice to a near whisper. He is ice cold as he says this, 'She left our wedding tonight, in front of all our family and friends.' He stops there, doesn't take it to any logical conclusion. But it gives me something to cling on to.

I run my hands through my hair. I am filled with a happy relief. Sun takes my hand and puts his phone in it. He whispers in my ear, 'You fool, you gave me the perfect insurance. The picture on this screen was sent to Public Security fifteen minutes ago. They are on their way.'

I look down. The image is of the man I bound up clumsily with the lamp cord. I am, of course, behind him. I stammer, disbelief giving way to anger as I realise what is really going on. 'You... you still fucking have him, don't you?' I have raised my voice and people close to us stare. An old lady moves away, clutching her luggage.

Sun leans back in his chair, snatches the phone back. 'Of course,' he whispers.

I stand up; I want to run. But I freeze, knowing there is nowhere to go, nothing I can do. Everything is over this time. I have set my own trap and it is closing around me.

Sun stands beside me, puts his hand on my shoulder and says, 'If you run, it will look even worse. Think of your dignity. It's all you have left now.'

*

Zhen

I rush through the terminal. Trying to figure out where Lindon could be. I am driven by anger, surfing a wave of it. One of the false eyelashes painstakingly glued to my face a few hours ago falls. I rip the other one off and throw them both over my shoulder as I see the sign for the international lounge. People stare and make a big effort to walk in arcs away from me, avoid meeting my eyes. A security guard approaches me cautiously, arms out to indicate I should stop but I scream at him, 'My husband, my dear husband cheated me!' and he backs off.

I slip on my stockings as I run across the perfect glassy floor. I don't notice the people staring at me any more. I just scan the lounges, desperate to see him. I start to get the demolished feeling he has left already, flown back to his country, the other end of the planet. Part of me feels like the wrecking ball is swinging closer. Tears cloud my eyes and I get angry at wasting them on a cheat like Lindon. I can see no sign of him. I scan the departures board and see no recent departure for Australia.

I turn round in a circle on the spot under the departure board making eye contact with everyone. Make-up runs down my face, the mask of my wedding dripping away. Spinning faster, the terminal starts to blur, faces become streaks and I fall against the board. I realise what a fool I must look. A lunatic.

I walk towards the duty-free shops, hoping he is lost in one of those. I see handbags worth more than my yearly salary. I curse money and the dirt it produces. I curse those who can afford to fly away from the dirt and leave us here.

It's then I see the mud. Airports are such shiny, glossy places but here on the white tiles under my feet is mud, streaks of it. I wipe my eyes and clear the tears, black smears of mascara on my hands. I crouch down and stare closely at the mud, touch it. Someone comes, someone else in uniform, and touches my shoulder. 'Miss, can I help you?'

I follow the mud with my eyes. It forms a trail back towards the entrance, out of the international terminal. I look up at the uniform. 'No, I think I'm OK.' This mud can only be him; it's our curse to share this stain. The guard grabs my shoulder, tries to pull me away from the trail. I swing round and, without great strength but with simple accuracy, kick him in a place that makes all men fall. He crumples and gasps.

I run out of the international terminal following the line of mud. It is composed of footprints that have become blurred with other peoples' steps intersecting the trail. It snakes out of the terminal and into a lounge near the main entrance, one I'd passed. The lounge is huge, inhumanely proportioned. As I stop to take stock of the space a cleaner pushes a long mop through the trail, and a glossy white floor is left in its wake. I open my mouth to cry out at the cleaner but the words fail me. I stand there on a clean floor, swamped in the stares of people who think I am mad. There are no tears. At that moment I feel tired and crushed. The way a defeated soldier must feel on a battlefield.

I fold my arms now, conscious of how I must look. I wish I had a coat or something to cover myself. I want to be shielded within something else. I feel small in this place, broken. I turn to go, spin on my cold feet on the hard clean floor. It's then that

I see them. They don't recognise me. I must look so insane they don't know who I am. They still walk like robots, but they are talking to someone on a phone and scanning the space: Lindon's two bodyguards are a few metres away; I recognise the expensive dark glasses, the robot walk. I turn, try and see where they are going but I can't recognise anyone walking in front of them.

I follow them, a safe small distance behind. They walk towards the back of the space, towards the wall of glass that looks out on the runway. It's then, between heads, that I see them and my heart ices over. I hesitate then, resist the urge I have to run at Lindon and beat him – Sun sits opposite him. He is whispering in Lindon's ear. I can't face Sun again, but I force myself to keep walking, driven by Lindon. I don't know if it is anger or the feeling I refuse to name.

The bodyguards reach the two of them, and they grab Lindon. Sun expresses no surprise, no alarm. He looks at one of them like they know each other. I run. I weave through people, jump over wheeled bags, bump into children. I pass a rack of books and I kick out. Books tumble on polished stone. A shop assistant runs after me. I kick at a stand of water bottles and they roll under people's feet. Security guards converge behind me.

I get to Lindon, people shouting behind me in anger. He looks shocked and doesn't see me; he just sees the chaos. I put my hand on his arm. Sun opens his mouth to say something to me and, as he does so, Lindon says, 'Zhen, he has him, he still has him.'

In one terrible moment the presence of the guards and Sun's manner over the last few days gel. It is Sun who is the real double-headed snake, not Lindon.

One of the guards lets go of Lindon and grabs my arm. His grip is firm, his fingers claw into my arm. I have one hand free and without thinking about it I use my only asset at that moment – my destitute state. I wave my hand and scream whatever I think will raise attention. Uniforms are around me. 'Xinjiang separatist! They have knives, extremists, they want to kill us all!' The bodyguards let go of both of us, stunned. Sun is the first to slither away, lost in the fleeing crowd, a rat deserting the sinking ship. Uniforms do descend rapidly and zero in on the bodyguards, who are grabbed by two uniformed men. Another takes hold of Lindon as he tries to step towards me. I manage to grip Lindon's clothing but the uniform tugs back and yells something incoherent at me. A small crowd presses in to watch us, some take pictures with their phones. As the uniform turns to lead Lindon away from me I use all my force to kick out at the back of his knee. He crumples, falls forwards into the crowd. Lindon and I run for the door, pushing bystanders away and using the confusion for cover. In the chaos we somehow get out.

Outside Lindon gives me his muddy coat, and immediately I am shielded from the cold. I spin round and slap him, throw my weight into it. He recoils, puts his hand to his face. He normally has something to say but he is silent. He just stares at me.

I attack him, feel the anger coming back. 'I left

my wedding for you, and you were with a whore. I don't care where you go, but I just wanted to tell you that. Tell you…' He opens his mouth to speak, but words don't come, and I press on. 'I'm telling you I will do my own thing now. You go, go back to Sydney or wherever you came from.' I turn my back on him, intending to walk away, but my feet don't do as I say.

'She was a whore, I think,' Lindon says quietly. I spin round and want to strike him again now, but he reaches out to hold my arm. 'But she wasn't *my* whore.'

I pull his coat around me. 'Likely story, all you foreigners.'

'It was a business dinner…' His voice trails off.

I look away from him. 'You are telling me stories.' But there is something about him that extinguishes my anger. He is Lindon, not a foreigner.

He runs his hand down my arm. 'I didn't want to be there. You know where I wanted to be. With you.'

We make eye contact. I search his eyes. I want to hold him, but I stay where I am, maintain my distance. Lindon's eyes are full of tears.

I say, 'My wedding, I—'

But it is then that I see one of the bodyguards. He must have got free of the uniforms. He has seen us and is making his way towards us. I grab Lindon's arm. 'We have to go. We have to go now!' We are lucky, there is a taxi next to us and we tumble in. I know where we need to go, and I tell the driver to drive quickly. Lindon and I start off sitting as far from each other on the back seat as we can. I fold my arms as we pull away and snap, 'What were you doing at an airport anyway?'

Lindon sighs. 'It's a good place to think, a long story. I hope you know where we are going now.' I begin to explain, and to do that I have to go back to my childhood.

*

Lindon

Zhen looks terrible, a wreck of smudged make-up, mud and salt stains from melting ice. I give her my shoes in the taxi and insist she wears them, at least for now, to warm her feet up. I want to ask about the wedding but I know it's not the time. Being with her now, like this, is still so impossible I feel numb. I have filled Zhen in on Sun's threat but she seems calm, thoughtful.

She has thrown a wad of cash at the driver to go quicker. She begins to unravel her childhood to me as the city rushes by. I'm so scared at the snaking and weaving we are doing around the traffic that I twist and watch Zhen, ignoring the windows. She says, 'In the mid-nineties there was a state of emergency. We were too young to understand what it was but there were whispers and rumours. My father didn't talk about it for years but admitted a decade later, when it was safe to talk, that there was a massive protest in the city. They lost control of the industrial area. There were many riots about unemployment. They were closing down one of the big state-owned plants.

This whole area was the centre of the movement. Some people said the workers actually took over the factory, I don't know the details.'

The taxi lurches suddenly to the left and I find myself pushed against her. I grip the handle above her window and slowly pull myself away, my body reluctant to leave her. I feel how cold her skin is. She shifts closer to me after that and starts to shiver. 'Sun and I were always close. I would tease him but he never teased me back. He'd look out for me, rescue me if I needed rescuing. We believed love comes slowly over time. I began to feel I loved him later. That day he pulled me out of class, told me there was great trouble outside and we ran from my house through rioters, he showed me a secret place. In the sixties they had built bomb shelters under major cities but they were mostly forgotten by the nineties, mistakes to be built over and left sleeping.'

The taxi arcs out in front of a small truck and lurches onto an exit ramp. I grab the handle again and press myself closer to Zhen; she doesn't pull away and her shivering starts to fade. I say, 'These bomb shelters, you still know how to get into them?'

She nods. 'Of course. And I think it's the only place Sun could have kept someone for a few days without suspicion. We played down there all the time when I was growing up. I had my first kiss there.'

The taxi screeches to a halt in front of the building site but Zhen barks some more directions at the driver who shrugs and pulls away from the curve again.

We round the back of the site and turn down some small lanes wide enough for only one vehicle. We are moving so swiftly we wouldn't have time to avoid a collision if someone were coming the other way.

Zhen asks the driver to stop and the taxi skids slightly and comes to rest at an unnatural angle in one of the lanes. I can see no doors, no gates, just old lane walls. Zhen jumps out quickly. She waits until the taxi pulls away and disappears around a corner before moving further down the narrow road. She grabs a large rock from the slush on the ground and tries to lob it at a streetlight but her dress constrains the movement of her arm so she rips it down the side. She gets her hand caught in the tear; I take the rock from her and throw it at the light but miss. She sighs, grabs another rock and despite the dress manages to hit it with her first throw and the lane goes dark.

I walk slowly with her – she is trying to go at a normal walking pace but in my oversized shoes she shuffles slowly through the slush.

'I can carry you if it's quicker,' I say as she stops, looks around.

'Not necessary. I don't think he would tell Public Security exactly where the guy is. That would make him look complicit. We need to have our heads clear and calm when we do find him.'

I imagine the complexity of these shelters and I have an idea for a distraction that could slow the police down, but it's dramatic and dangerous.

I explain my idea to Zhen. She stops, examines my face as if calculating and then nods slowly. 'It might buy us more time, and create a big problem for them.'

I forestall her next question. 'There will be no one there. But I can set off alarms to make sure. It will just be a distraction. A big distraction.'

She takes in a lungful of air, her eyes wide. 'That must be what you call "understatement" in English!'

I gulp, try to look calm but I grab her hand to take her with me. I will need her to still my nerves. We run back towards the site office, giddy, my stomach churning with nervous energy.

VI

Zhen

We make our way back to the alley from the site, our gamble to slow down the police now set in motion. Lindon seems convinced it will be safe, but I have a sense we can't control it. There is no time to think, only to do. I stop by a drain in the road and I get him to drag the metal grate away from its entrance. My hands sting in the cold water melted around it. Lindon heaves the cover off, and it scrapes the surface of the road. We hesitate, make sure no one sees us and Lindon disappears down the hole first. It's narrow, and as I follow I battle down the rusty ladder.

It's dark at the bottom, wet. Icy water covers my shoes and spills around my feet. I get out my phone and push Lindon out of the way so that I can lead. I see his face light in the dim glow and allow myself to feel what I have been pushing down all along. I am, for the first time, gripped by fear.

I turn and use the phone to illuminate my face so he can see me and say, 'It will be warmer soon, stay close.' The light from the phone helps me to locate a large metal handle. I pull open a door, and warmer air does rush out at us. My feet begin to warm as we walk, the sound of our breathing echoing off the walls.

'Explain,' – I break the silence, hope the talk will distract me, dull the fear – 'the airport. I know you were doing more than just thinking.' He lets two or three steps fall before answering.

'I did think about getting on a plane. That is true.'

I put out my hand to stop him at a junction. I remember following this path with Sun. Having Lindon with me here is like rewiring these memories, replacing Sun somehow. I feel like I am betraying a memory, but I feel Lindon behind me, it reassures me.

I tell him to continue. He clears his throat. His voice is soft, fragile. 'Once when I was a kid... at primary school, I was walking home with a mate and we were jumped by three older boys. We were smaller, had never done any training or fighting before. But I was a little bigger-looking, and they really wanted my friend. I'm not sure why. Maybe it was his glasses, I don't know...' We make another couple of turns. I feel memories pressing in on me, the past smudging the present.

Lindon continues, 'When they started pushing my mate I took a swing. The oldest attacker simply pushed me over and when I jumped back up he laughed – he was so much taller he could hold me at a distance and my fists couldn't even make contact with his body. I had to watch while my mate was beaten. All I could do was mop up the blood when it was over.'

I stop, shine my phone at him. I am flushed with irritation. 'Is China the bully in this story?' My eyebrows arch up at him.

He looks down at the darkness of the ground below searching for an answer. 'Haven't you ever felt that sense of powerlessness? That no matter what you do the punches land on someone and there is nothing you can do to help?'

I let the phone fall by my side. He is shrouded in darkness. I can smell the staleness of this place now. It smells like it is rotting, sinking into the earth. All I can think to do is touch Lindon's arm but as I do I hear a voice yell to us. I am startled, almost drop the phone as the sound echoes around us.

I quickly lead Lindon through another open door near us to where the voice has come from. I know that if I had shone the phone up to the door frame as we passed I would have seen the characters of my name Sun etched there all those years ago. A lifetime ago. But I don't want to see them. I want to forget.

There is a lamp on in the room, and I recognise the man Lindon tied up days ago in our house. He is sitting on a chair, and yells at us. At the back of the room there is a box of bottled water and packets of junk food. I wonder why he hasn't wandered off but then I see he has been attached to a door on the other side of the room with a thin chain. He looks, our prisoner, like a dog in a backyard.

I'm startled by a noise from a corner beside me and out of the corner shuffles a man I don't recognise until he smiles and I see perfect white teeth – and behind him, my father. As they get closer I realise the man is Mr Hu, one of my father's friends. I just stare. My father must see my confusion, know how it looks.

My father puts up his hands. 'I didn't know, little Zhen.'

Mr Hu shuffles forwards, eyes wide. 'Public Security have been looking around for a missing man. Your father is clever, he smelt a rat with your fiancé – former fiancé.'

I look from one to the other. I search their faces for the truth. I know my father wouldn't lie to me. I have to trust him now. I check my phone for a mobile signal. I have one bar.

'How did you know about this place?' I ask my father. I had thought this was Sun's and my secret, something hidden and buried. It feels like our past is naked in front of them all.

My father and Mr Hu laugh. 'You youngsters think you know everything. We used to come down here on drills. We know you played here. We wouldn't have let you play here alone.'

I wonder what else they know about me. But my father changes the subject, his face set with worry.

'We need to get this man to the police. He will tell them about Sun for us.'

Mr Hu looks exasperated. 'We have been arguing about this. I have been telling your father how foolish he is. Your father thinks everyone is good. When he goes to the police, this man will lie. His truth is for sale.'

My father sighs. I translate what has taken place to Lindon, who now speaks. 'I think Mr Hu is probably right. There are big amounts of money involved in this project. Money does strange things to people.'

The prisoner pulls on the chain and swears at us. 'Please just let me go. I won't tell anyone about anything! I have a daughter waiting for me at home; she doesn't know where I am...'

Mr Hu mutters under his breath, 'Cow's cunt,' and shakes his head, 'No'.

My father waves us all to a corner away from the prisoner, who tugs his chain and yells, 'Don't leave me. Come on. Stay.'

'He shouldn't hear this,' my father says, and we go through the doorway at the far end of the room and head into the corridor. Mr Hu grabs the lamp as he follows us, leaving the prisoner in darkness. The man screams as Mr Hu seals the door behind us. Lindon grimaces, his face drained of colour.

Mr Hu whispers now. 'I have a plan. I have a way out for you and the foreigner here.' Lindon drags his eyes away from the door and listens intently to my translation; he seems desperate to hear any option.

I think of the fire Lindon and I started, look at my phone to see what the time is, and wonder how long it will take to do its job. Danger is creeping up on us, is close. Mr Hu continues, 'Your father and I are old, finished. They won't be too hard on us. The company has been trying to bully you out of your home for months. We might do some time but it won't be long, not with so much trouble about these buildings—'

I shake my head, cut him off. 'I can't let you two take the blame, I can't. Sun got us into this and he will be brought to justice. I won't let you.' I reach for the phone but my father yells at me, 'Stop. Zhen, stop.'

I turn back around slowly. My father takes my wrist gently, strokes it. 'There is more to the plan. It is a good one, it is a way out.'

I look from my father to Mr Hu. There are more sirens now. They are punctuated by the sound of kids playing with fireworks again, bangs like gunfire. It's unnerving, makes me flinch. Our fire can't have taken hold; nothing has happened. I am anxious about this but feel a weight lift from my shoulders at the same time. Mr Hu says, 'It wouldn't work if we took the blame for it. Sun would get around us. I—' He looks at my father, who nods. 'We know a way to make this work for us, a way that would be trouble enough that would get us into the papers as well. Everyone would talk about it. It would give us a chance.'

The prisoner screams again. He must have heard

the sirens and he is shouting for help. It is hard to make out exactly what he is yelling but it sounds like accusations against us. Mr Hu was right. He would betray us all with a series of lies. I am comforted knowing how thick the concrete is here, and that no one will hear him from above. But it is unnerving.

Mr Hu says, 'Your father and I will kidnap you and the foreigner. We will chain you with the man in there, the traitor. You will be our hostages.'

I stare at them for a few seconds, stunned. I feel sweat run down my back, my chest tight with the pressure of this on me. I breathe a bit harder, grapple for air. Lindon squeezes my hand, waiting for a translation but I don't know what to say. My father nods at me, says, 'It will work. The TV and the newspapers will love the story. You will say how we treated you with respect, that we did it only to make our story reach the world.'

Lindon hears the translation and grips my arm. 'Your father will go to prison even if they gain sympathy. Surely we can't condemn them to prison. This is all my fault. If I had stood up to Frank, we might not be in this situation.'

My father demands a translation of Lindon's comment and replies, 'If you had confronted anyone in the company, you would have been on a plane back to where you came from!'

Mr Hu says, 'Our plan is the only way. And,' – he points at Lindon – 'this is a way your white skin can actually do some good.' He moves forwards to grab Lindon but I step between them. I have never fought before but I clench my fists tight, ready for violence.

Lindon says to me, 'He is right.'

I crouch down, my legs suddenly heavy with tiredness, my feet sore. 'Whatever we do, we have to decide quickly. The longer we delay the more it could be argued we were involved. I know it's a risk, but we have to let him go, present him to the police. We could look like rescuers.' I still have one bar showing on my phone. I scroll through to find the number of local Public Security.

Mr Hu watches me, frightened. 'What are you doing with your phone? We have a plan.' He reaches out to grab it and Lindon tries to come between us. My father pulls Mr Hu back but he is strong and Lindon is off balance.

'Everyone just calm down!' I yell at them. I pull free with my father's help, and step back. 'I'm calling the police.'

Lindon lunges forwards now, grabs my father's arm. 'We need to get away from here quickly. There will be time later to talk more.' I can see he is anxious about the fire burning somewhere above us, but it should have taken hold by now; it should have done its job. Sirens sound closer, pressing in on us. My father takes a moment to process the English but must have grasped the gist because he moves with Lindon. Mr Hu stands where he is, unsure. My phone signal is weak but it begins to connect. I turn back to Mr Hu and ask him to get the prisoner and he turns slowly, reluctantly. As we walk ahead I hear a weak, scratchy dial tone. Just as I get through, we all hear a voice from our left in the darkness, a voice that freezes us to the spot.

'Zhen, come home with me.' It is Sun. We all look over at him, and he adds, 'The police are on their way, everything will be OK now. We can forget about the foreigner...'

My father tries to block Sun and me but I push him aside. I hear the police on the other end of the phone, but I hang up. I step towards Sun. He has a small torch and I can see that his hand is stretched out towards me. I say to Lindon and my father, 'Keep going, we don't have time. Go!' But Sun pulls out a knife. He holds the blade out parallel to the beam from the torch. Its silvery reflection cuts the darkness open, bleeds flashes of light.

'No one is going anywhere. We are going to wait right here until the police arrive.' He says this in Chinese and then English. It feels like everything has slowed down. I can hear my heart pounding in my head, my throat.

Lindon – I see his face dimly in the light from Sun's torch – has lost any colour he had in his face. I see panic growing in his eyes, devouring him from the inside. He is sweating now.

'We can deal with this outside,' he says. 'We need to get away from here, a safe distance. We have started a fire near the—'

Sun lunges forwards and grabs the edge of my dress, holds it, cuts Lindon off. 'I don't want anyone to get hurt, we can talk *here*.' The knife is near me now. I look from his face to the knife and back, trying to reconcile Sun with the blade thrust at me.

Sun snaps at Lindon, 'You have no right to speak. You have done enough damage to us.'

Lindon raises his hands in submission, nods in agreement.

I say, 'How can you do this? You are a coward!'

Sun speaks quickly, 'I won't hurt you Zhen, I'll never hurt you. I just don't want you to run. We can become what we were.'

I look into his eyes, search them for the Sun I know. 'How can things go backwards?'

'I am still the same man. I have to provide for you. What kind of a man would I be if I didn't?'

I squint at Sun. 'You betrayed what you were.'

Sun grits his teeth, points the knife at me. 'Do you think running away with him,' – he points the knife at Lindon – 'is who *you* are? Running when things get tough while I *work* us out of our situation?'

I grasp the blade, cutting my hand open. I wince at the pain but pull the knife back to me and point it at my own chest. I feel Sun's grip weaken, his eyes widen. I see the whites clearly in the inky black around us. 'I am not running. I am following this,' – I pull the knife against my dress over my heart, feel its sharpness press against me through the fabric – 'like I thought you used to.'

Sun smirks and opens his mouth to respond. As he does I pull my dress away, feel it tear. I lunge towards the door, push my father aside. It is then that the ground shudders. The gods themselves seem to tear at us. We are thrown across the room. It's as if the world is ending, collapsing around us. Our fire must have taken hold, must have finally heated up those LPG tanks enough. The earth itself shakes. Giant jaws of concrete threaten to devour us all.

*

Lindon

I have always wondered what death would be like. These thoughts have sometimes been frightening, terrifying even; other times gently curious, almost playful. I used to hold my breath as a kid in my bed and hope that this would take me to the edge, to the frontier that separates life and death. Of course it never did. We will all know what death is like but few of us will ever get the feeling we have come back from the brink. But now, as the floor shakes and debris begins to fall, I think this is it.

I shield my face with my hands, my heart pounding in my chest. There is no thinking involved, it's all adrenaline, reflex and terror. My eyes and mouth are filled with dust and dirt, I begin to choke as my nose and my throat fill with dry, sickly air. I begin to panic as it becomes harder to inhale. The ground rattles again and I am pushed further away from where I was originally thrown. It feels like the walls themselves are threatening to collapse, to bury us in the earth. I finally begin to realise what death is like and I don't want to be here any more. I feel frail, brittle, the most afraid I have ever been.

And then, suddenly, it stops. I can see nothing for a while; the air is still thick with dust. The room, what is left of it, is now a jagged space I don't recognise. I squint up and see distant flames illuminating everything in licks of orange and yellow. It's hot when I stand up amongst giant bones of rock. I shrink away from the heat, find somewhere cooler under a slab of concrete.

I'm flooded with panic for Zhen. I try to call out her name but my throat is still full of dust. I cough as I try to yell, choke on what I had sucked in and vomit suddenly at my feet. I double over with my hands on my thighs. I retch again but I find it easier to breathe now. I hear someone else being sick off to my left, recognise the voice of Zhen's dad. I try to get towards him but can't. My way is blocked by a fallen slab.

I call out Zhen's name now I have my voice. It echoes off the pieces of shattered room I'm entombed in. When I stop to listen I hear the sound of fire. It sounds like rain, like a tropical storm. I start to sweat as the heat floods the air. I hear another voice, a man's voice; I don't know who it is but it is calm, measured. Zhen's dad calls his daughter's name, but there are only flames, growing heat. His desperate shouts seem to get closer and then he appears behind me, on his knees. They have crawled through a space behind me and Zhen's father stands beside me now. Mr Hu crouches beside us wiping dust and grit from his eyes but otherwise he seems okay. Zhen's father checks me over and gives me the thumbs up. I hadn't even checked myself for wounds, for blood. I only thought of Zhen.

He calls Zhen's name again as I look for another small opening, a way to see more of the space. I notice another gap and I squeeze through it, dragging myself under jagged shapes. I stop occasionally to listen for her, to call out her name. Sweat saturates my clothes, rains off my face and blinds me with salty waves of tears.

As panic begins to crash over me I feel a hand on my back, and I spin round and see her smile, see her eyes glow in the darkness. She is squatting on the ground, her phone glowing in her hand. I kiss her softly on the lips, taste concrete and mud and grit but it is the softest kiss. The petals of her lips discovered amongst fire and heat. Zhen stops me, pushes me back. 'My father?'

I just smile and nod, watch her shoulders relax. She wipes some mud from her face and it smears across her cheeks, her nose. Her hair is grey with dust. She sniffs the air and looks up. 'We were under your office, too close to the LPG tanks…'

It explains the intense heat, the severity of the explosion. I can't begin to imagine the damage it's done to the site.

Zhen stands, checks herself for wounds, broken bones. We have all been lucky, but I can hear nothing from Sun. We start calling for Zhen's father and we crawl towards his voice.

Zhen hugs her father, asks him if he has seen Sun. He tells her something in Chinese and she looks at me, her eyes wide and empty, her mouth slack. I don't need her to say what he has told her, that Sun is dead. I am numb, don't know what to say or what to do, but the heat presses in on us, keeps me focused on immediate danger. Zhen lets go of her father and falls on her hands and knees. I see tears spill out over her face. She comes over to me and stops in front of me. She looks at me, her hair grey and dirty and partially covering her moist eyes. I move the hair across. If I am to die here now, trapped in this tomb, at least I have found what's worth being here for. She holds me and we are swallowed by our silence.

The heat intensifies, starts to make it hard to breath. I can see sweat pouring off her father's face. The rubble seems to press in on me now, drown my senses. Will we get out?

Zhen's father says, 'We are very lucky.'

Zhen sniffs. 'We are not so lucky. We will die slowly in this heat. Cooked like dumplings.'

Her father nods back behind us, says calmly, 'I did see something that looks like a way out behind you. We will not die today, little Zhen.'

I think about what Zhen said, and realise for the

first time that we do have a way out of this, a very different way out from the literal one her father has spotted. It seems to be the only way for her family to have any peace, for Zhen to get her new life. It is so simple my mouth falls open and I stare up to where the flames are above us. Zhen looks at me like I've gone mad, lost my mind.

I clear my mouth and look down at them both, look them each in the eye. I tell them to listen very carefully, and to take time to think about what I say before they speak. I begin with, 'The way out has been presented to us.' I wipe sweat from my face, out of my eyes. 'Sun is dead, he no longer has a story. The company will no doubt want to use me as a scapegoat for what's happened above—'

Zhen cuts me off. 'How can you be held responsible?'

'I was the project manager. The buck stops with me. But this fire,' – I point above and feel the heat it produces – 'we can use that fire. They need a sacrifice up there, a neat loose end to pin the blame on. I have to die, I have to die in that fire.'

Epilogue

Zhen

I read about Lindon's death in the *People's Daily*.
The train passed Xian a few hours ago and is now
well into the deserts of Gansu. I can see dusty tan
hills and spider webs of valley cut into them. It has
an eerie deathly beauty to it. I have never felt so free.

The article talks about the valour of three Public
Security officers hurt in the explosion and devotes a
paragraph to the 'foreign manager who died in his
office while trying to help coordinate the search for
the missing man'. The company must have paid a lot
of money for that lie. The story ends with the news
that Beijing have sent investigators to look into the
case, to 'root out corrupt practice in the city that
this case has brought to light'. There is no mention
of Sun's death. He has been erased from the story,
buried under the foundations. Despite everything I
feel a pang of pity for him.

I throw the newspaper onto the empty seat beside me and smell the tea I'm drinking before I sip it. I close my eyes and am conscious only of the sweetness of the tea and the gentle rattle of the high-speed train. An unwanted image intrudes now, pushes its way into the darkness and sours the smell of the tea. It is Sun. I see him as he was a long time ago. Time reversed, something pure poured back into him, made new. He smiles at me, picks out the best piece of meat from a steaming plate of pork and gives it to me. I roll the pork around in my mouth, can taste the fatty bits of it. I feel tears start to form and I am afraid to open my eyes. My heart aches for that Sun, the Sun who died *before* the explosion, a long time before. I have grieved for Sun many times over now, but his physical death is the easiest. I feel guilt for that, shame.

I open my eyes and the desert is a blur, I can't even see Tianshi now. I wipe away the evidence of my grief with an old tissue. I struggle to bring the mountains into focus.

I feel the presence of someone beside me and I start, the price of being a fugitive. I sniff and dab at my eyes again.

'Police. If you could show me your ID please...' I hit Lindon as he finishes his joke. He has food balanced on a tray, piles of steaming rice and vegetables. I still haven't quite got used to the red colour he put through his hair at the station. It's startling how different it makes him. There are messy streaks he missed, traces of the old colour showing through. He passes me the tray, then sits and looks into my eyes. He can see the signs of my tears and he wants to say something. I can see him searching for words, but all he can do is put his hand on my arm. It makes me smile, but fresh tears muddle my happiness. He gets me more tissues and I turn as we watch the desert together.

After some time he says quietly, 'Are you sure about this? Coming out here?'

I see Sun with the knife, see the death in his eyes. I turn to Lindon, the tears drying on my cheeks. 'We can't go back now that you are "dead".'

He frowns at me. I see the western desert reflected in his eyes. I rub his arm and his frown fades. I feel more tears coming but I have a sense they are washing away something.

'If this is what death is for us, it's good. I won't mourn the loss of that life. In a few months we can meet my parents somewhere out here. My mother would love the desert. She would say it was "strengthening", builds strong revolutionary spirit.'

Lindon is quiet a while more, watches me. Then he says, 'I'm happier now with nothing than I was before when I was trying to fill a bank account up.'

I slap him softly. 'You saying I'm nothing?'

He seems to relax, tension starts to dissolve from around his eyes. 'You are my blue desert sky. Everywhere.'

Love is war. It's a series of tactical responses, to conquer and to vanquish your enemy. If you don't defend yourself, your body will be defeated. Life is guerrilla war, a constant struggle. You have to know when to retreat and when to attack. You have to know when to harass a retreating enemy, and you have to know when to disappear.

We are so focussed on winning we don't ask ourselves what a 'victory' really is. And that can be harder than the fight itself.

For some people victory is an apartment, a car and a bank account. But not for me.

Lindon pulls me close. I see old houses with adobe walls by the railway tracks, a sign we will reach Lanzhou soon, a silk road city growing taller out the desert – a place where they are literally moving mountains to build a new city next to the old. A new life will sprout here for us form the waters of the Yellow River that runs through the city. No more mud for us. A place to begin to forget old faces. Just the jewel of never-ending desert sky.

Life from death. I try not to cry.

Acknowledgements

Thanks to my wonderful reader group, who kept me going through the early and mid-stages and helped the story and characters grow: Peter Jackson, Peter Rotundo, Yunan Chen, Huang Yan Ting (Jen), Dr Judith Smyth, Jennifer Tang, Duncan Weller, Paul Sainty, Nigel Pritchard and Yu Xiaofang. A special thank you to Rashmi Jolly for in-depth discussions on the characters and working with me on plotting in those critical planning stages. Thanks also to the team at Fairlight Books (Louise, Urška and Lindsey, in particular) who have been a pleasure to work with. It's been a very positive experience and I am grateful for your work. A thank you also to Charlotte for her editing work. I particularly love the covers for this series – they do all the work justice.

I was inspired over the course of writing this book by two wonderful novels, *The Girl Who Played Go* by Shan Sa, and *A Concise Chinese-English Dictionary for Lovers* by Xiaolu Guo. The music of

Radiohead and the solo work of Thom Yorke have been constant musical companions.

A special thanks to my mother for her encouragement. She has been a role model – proof that you are never too old or too young to do the things that are important. We all have our own timelines. Thanks to my father for a sense of hunger to see the world and encouraging us to make sure life has enough adventure in it.

It would be very difficult to write and work full-time without the support of my wonderful family, who live with my daydreaming and understand when I hunch over a screen lost in thought from time to time. My wife and I met and fell in love in China and had our two children there, so writing this novel is very much a product of that adventure. This book belongs to you three very beautiful people. Words aren't good enough to tell you how important you are to me.

Bookclub and writers' circle notes for the
Fairlight Moderns can be found at
www.fairlightmoderns.com

Share your thoughts about the
book with **#NailHouse**

Also in the Fairlight Moderns series

SOPHIE VAN LLEWYN

Bottled Goods

*Longlisted for **The Women's Prize for Fiction 2019**,
People's Book Prize for Fiction 2018 and **The Republic
of Consciousness Prize 2019***

When Alina's brother-in-law defects to the West,
she and her husband become persons of interest to
the secret services and both of their careers come
grinding to a halt.

As the strain takes its toll on their marriage,
Alina turns to her aunt for help – the wife of a
communist leader and a secret practitioner of the
old folk ways.

Set in 1970s communist Romania, this novella-
in-flash draws upon magic realism to weave a
captivating tale of everyday troubles.

*'It is a story to savour, to smile at, to
rage against and to weep over.'*
—Zoe Gilbert, author of *FOLK*

*'Sophie van Llewyn's stunning debut novella
shows us there is no dystopian fiction as
frightening as that which draws on history.'*
— Christina Dalcher, author of *VOX*

OMAR SABBAGH

Minutes from the Miracle City

Hakim, a Pakistani taxi driver whizzing through
the streets. Patrick, a Ugandan security guard
with aspirations of becoming a writer. Farida, a
Moroccan beautician hoping for a fresh start.
Saeed, a respected Emirati journalist just back from
London.

Taking place across the last few days of Ramadan,
Minutes from the Miracle City is a fresh and unique
retelling of the virtuoso project that is Dubai.

*'Sabbagh gives us something we do not
expect: a small place packed with complex
dwellers.'*
—Adnan Mahmutović, author of
How to Fare Well and Stay Fair

'Sabbagh is the RK Narayan of our times.'
—Christopher Jackson,
poet and biographer

NIAL GIACOMELLI

The Therapist

'*I am levitating above the curvature of the earth.
Weightless, unencumbered. Flung like a comet out of
the atmosphere and into some great beyond.*'

In this bittersweet and hauntingly surreal tale, a
couple finds the distance between them mirrored
in a strange epidemic sweeping the globe. Little by
little, each victim becomes transparent, their heart
beating behind a visible rib cage, an intricate
network of nerves left hanging in mid-air. Finally,
the victims disappear entirely, never to be
seen again.

'I dreamt we were at sea,' she says.

Praise for the *Fairlight Moderns:*

'*If the population of the world had vanished
while I was reading Nial Giacomelli's
beautifully observed novella, I'm not sure
I would have noticed. It's that good.*
—Christopher Stanley, author of
The Forest is Hungry